Pets RULE!

My Kingdom of Darkness

Read all the Pets RULE! books

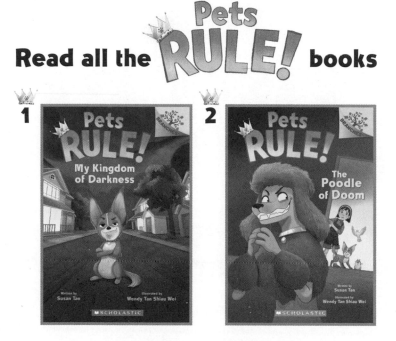

Get your paws on book #3, too!

My Kingdom
of Darkness

Written by
Susan Tan

Illustrated by
Wendy Tan Shiau Wei

SCHOLASTIC INC.

To rescue dogs and the humans who love them. – ST

To Lucky, you're my sweetie pie! – WTSW

Text copyright © 2022 by Susan Tan
Illustrations copyright © 2022 by Wendy Tan Shiau Wei

First edition. | New York: Scholastic Inc., 2022. | Series: Pets rule; 1 | Summary: For Ember, a rescue Chihuahua and the newest pet in the Chin family, the first step in fulfilling his destiny to rule the world is to defeat the evil neighborhood squirrel, Masher. Identifiers: LCCN 2021013035 | ISBN 9781338756333 (paperback) | ISBN 9781338756340 (hardcover) Subjects: CYAC: Chihuahua (Dog breed)—Fiction. | Dogs—Fiction. | Squirrels—Fiction. | Pets—Fiction. | Bullies—Fiction. Classification: LCC PZ7.1.T37 My 2022 | DDC [Fic]—dc23 LC record available at https://lccn.loc.gov/2021013035

10 9 8 7 6 5 4 3 2 1   22 23 24 25 26

Printed in China   62
First edition, June 2022
Edited by Rachel Matson
Cover design by Maria Mercado
Book design by Jaime Lucero

Table of Contents

CHAPTER 1

Evil Set Free

For ages I have waited.

Locked away.

I knew that one day, the bars of my prison would open. And evil would walk free.

"At last. All will tremble before me!" I barked.

I looked around my new kingdom. Strangers towered over me.

"Greetings, humans," I said. "Fear me! Soon this kingdom will be mine."

But my new humans didn't understand.

"He's so small!" a boy with a baseball hat said.

"Look at his little ears!" a woman with glasses said.

"Bow, you fools," I said. "I am your future ruler."

"Listen to his tiny bark," the tallest one said.

"My bark isn't tiny," I said. "It is MAGNIFICENT and it will be heard across this land."

"Awwww," the boy said.

That's when I realized that these were not the smartest humans.

Except for the smallest one.

"He has a lot to say," she said quietly.

And I do.

You see, I am not an ordinary Chihuahua. I have a great and terrible destiny.

Normal Chihuahua:

Thinks about: DINNER!

Loves: His family

Enjoys: Chasing sticks

ME: Thinks about: WORLD DOMINATION

Loves: POWER!

Enjoys: Destroying his ENEMIES!!

Someday, I will rule the world. It is not going to be easy. First, I have to take over this house. I will make these humans my minions, which means they'll do everything I tell them to do.

Once I rule this house, I will build my pet army. And then, I will unleash my dark plans on the world. *BWAHAHAHAHAHA!*

Unfortunately, though, *leashes* are a BIG thing here.

And it's hard to make your minions fear you when you're wearing one. Especially when the leash is decorated with flowers.

"You'll pay for this," I told the tall one on our first walk.

"You're so cute," he said.

"I am not cute!" I barked. "I am EVIL."

But the minion didn't hear me.

After the walk, my minions tried to feed me dinner. But it wasn't up to my standards.

Before bed, the smallest human came to the kitchen and took a drawing down from the refrigerator. She sat next to me on the floor.

"This is your new family, puppy," she said. She showed me the drawing. "I'm Lucy. I'm going to be a famous geologist someday. That means someone who studies rocks and the earth. And this is my dad, my mom, and my brother, Kevin. We're the Chin family," she said.

"Excellent," I said. "You will be my minions, and I will reward you for serving me."

"Bedtime, Lucy," Mr. Chin said, coming into the kitchen.

"Can I take him to my room? I promise he'll behave," Lucy said.

"No, Lucy, we agreed. No dogs on the beds. He sleeps here," her dad said.

"Listen to Lucy, minion," I barked up at Mr. Chin. "Or you'll regret it."

7

"See?" Mr. Chin said, smiling. "He's getting used to things already."

I sighed and darted away as he tried to pat me.

I did let Lucy scratch my ears, though.

"Sorry, puppy," she said. "Good night. I'll see you in the morning."

Lucy closed the door to my crate. Mr. Chin turned off the light, and they went upstairs.

I was left all alone in a new prison, in a dark kitchen.

But I am used to the dark.

"It won't be long now," I said to the shadows. "Soon, I will rule this place."

I fell asleep and dreamed of evil deeds.

And I wasn't lonely or scared at all.

CHAPTER 2

Thunder Roads and Evil Trash Cans

I woke to the sound of thunder.

"Hurricane!" I cried.

But it was only the sound of my minions coming down the stairs.

"I'll take you for a walk," Lucy said, opening the door of my prison. "I know the leash is a pain. It's just to keep you safe."

10

"Thank you for your concern, minion," I said. "But I am pure evil. I fear nothing."

I didn't argue anymore, though, because the small minion has been kind to me.

Even though I hated the leash, it was nice to have Lucy close by. Outside, large metal creatures zoomed by on wheels. And worst of all, there were huge plastic giants who were *definitely* up to something.

I darted away from one of the giants. "Don't worry," Lucy said. "It's just a trash can."

"That's what they want you to think. When I'm in charge of the neighborhood, there will be NO *trash cans* allowed," I said.

Lucy and I went inside. Mr. Chin was making toast, and Kevin and Mrs. Chin were at the table eating breakfast.

"We still need to name him," Lucy said.

Mr. Chin handed her a piece of toast, and she took it to the table.

"Excellent idea," I said. "I suggest *Your Darkness* or *The All-Seeing Evil One*."

"Didn't the animal shelter name him?" Kevin asked between bites.

I whirled toward him.

"I warn you, minion," I said. "Do not say that unspeakable name."

"Yeah, but it's *terrible*," Lucy said.

"Exactly," I said. "Listen to the tiny one."

"I think it's sweet," Mrs. Chin said.

"No," I cried. "I am the opposite of sweet. DON'T SAY IT!"

But I couldn't stop them.

I watched in horror as Mr. Chin spoke.

"At the shelter," he said, "they named him '*Chuckles.*' I think it's kind of cute."

"NOOOOOOOOO," I howled.

As I'm sure you can see, if anything stands in the way of my destiny of world domination, it's being called *Chuckles.*

"It doesn't fit him at all," Lucy said. She waved her toast in the air. "Look, he doesn't like it!"

"Well, we will decide on his name later," Mrs. Chin said. "Now, you two need to get to school."

Lucy finished her toast quickly. She jumped up and grabbed her bag. Before she left, she stopped to kneel beside me.

"Bye, puppy," she said, scratching my fur. Then she leaned closer and whispered, "I promise I won't let them call you 'Chuckles.'"

"Thank you. You are my favorite minion," I whispered back.

Lucy, Kevin, and Mrs. Chin walked out to the car.

"I'll be back to walk you this afternoon," Mr. Chin said. He set up another gate, this one across the door of the kitchen.

And just like that, I was alone again, trapped by another prison gate.

All alone.

Except . . .

"Psst!"

I jumped, turning around. There was no one there.

"Pssst!" I heard again. And then.

Scrich scrich scrich.

"Who's there?" I asked. There was no answer.

Suddenly, the bars of the prison gate began to inch forward, pushed by an invisible hand.

I crept closer . . . and two giant eyes stared back at me.

CHAPTER 3

A Ruler Meets His Subjects

A monster!" I cried. I jumped back.

The creature came through the opening in the gate. It was headed straight for me. A terrible smell filled the room.

I tripped over my paws and fell. When I looked up, I was face-to-face with the creature. I saw two eyes in a giant mound of fur.

17

"Hi," the monster said. "I'm Steve. Do you have any food?"

"Who . . . who are you?" I asked. I stood up and tried to look like I wasn't scared. Evil creatures like me are not scared of anyone.

"I'm Steve, Kevin's hamster! Didn't the Chins tell you?" he asked. "There are other pets here. We're excited to meet you!"

"I am not a pet," I said. "I am the future ruler of this place. Dark Lord, Evil One—"

"Oh cool!" Steve said. "I like rulers. Once I got to chew on Kevin's old ruler from elementary school—delicious!"

This pet is not very smart, I thought. *But that's PERFECT. He will be my first subject!*

But I didn't say any of that out loud.

"Not that kind of ruler," I said. "I mean I will *rule* this house, and you will be my subject, which means you are a pet who will serve me. But when I'm in charge, you can chew on all the wooden rulers you like."

"Excellent!" Steve said.

"What about me?" a new voice asked. I looked up, and saw a bright yellow shape flying toward me.

"AH! GET DOWN! ENEMIES ARE COMING FROM THE SKIES!" I dove to the floor.

But Steve just stood there. "Hey, Neo," he said.

The creature fluttered to the floor. It seemed much smaller now that it had landed.

"Hi," she chirped at me. "I'm Neo the canary! Named for *neon* because I'm bright like a light. Welcome to the house." She said all this very fast.

"Uhhh," I said.

"Yeah," Steve added. "The Chins have fun with names. My full name is Smelly Steve Chin."

I blinked at him, feeling dread creep over me. Maybe I was going to be named "Chuckles" after all.

"Kevin named me this because my cage smells. And"—he lowered his voice like he was sharing a secret—"I think I kind of smell, too."

"Hello! I'm BeBe!" a tiny voice cried.

I jumped and turned around. No one was there.

Neo stretched out her wing.

"Look here," Neo said. She pointed with her beak. There, on her feathers, sat a very tiny black bug.

"I'm BeBe the beetle!" the bug called out in a tiny voice. "Nice to meet you."

"BeBe lives in the fern plant in Mr. and Mrs. Chin's bedroom," Neo said. "But I gave her a ride so she could meet you."

"A SPY," I said, hopping in excitement. "You could sneak into any place and no one would see you!"

I puffed my chest out and looked over my three newest minions.

"With your help, I'll soon rule this kingdom. Then all the kingdoms of this world," I said.

But my minions didn't seem excited. In fact, they looked worried.

"Uh-oh," BeBe said from Neo's back.

"Look, new pet," Neo said. "You're welcome to rule our house. But here's the thing. Someone already runs the neighborhood."

"Someone *bad*," Steve said, shuddering.

"*Who?*" I demanded. "WHO DARES?"

Neo's voice was hushed. "It's better if we show you."

CHAPTER 4

Masher Equals Bad News

I have seen some horrible things in my time. Things like trash cans.

Things like people who wear white coats and call themselves "vets."

But I have never seen anything as terrible as the thing I saw out the window.

Neo and Steve looked through with me. Their faces were serious and scared.

"There he is," Steve whispered.

The biggest, meanest squirrel I had ever seen was standing outside in the yard.

His teeth were sharp like spikes.

His tail looked like it could knock down trees.

His eyes shone with meanness.

And he was surrounded by squirrels. They were *everywhere*—on every tree branch.

"He's the meanest squirrel in the world," Steve said.

"UNACCEPTABLE!" I shouted. "*I* am the ruler of this place!"

"Shhh, he'll hear you!!" Steve whispered, tugging at my ear with his paw.

"I don't care!" I yelled.

"Hush, new guy," Steve said. "You don't know what Masher can do. He's a pet squirrel. And his human, Jimmy, is the meanest kid in Lucy's class."

"Jimmy always picks on Lucy," Neo said. "He's *awful*. She's shy anyway, and with Jimmy living right around the corner, it's even worse. And Masher is just as bad."

"Yeah, he loves acorns, and there aren't many acorn trees on our block. So he takes all the acorns and hides them in his secret stash. All the pets have to bring him acorns, and if we don't . . ." Steve stopped talking.

"If you don't, what happens?" I asked.

"Well, let's just say there's a reason he's called 'Masher,'" Neo said.

As if he heard us, Masher's tail began to thump against the ground.

I had seen enough.

"I will deal with this," I said. "Open the gate to our kingdom, Smelly Steve."

"No, new guy! Don't do it," Neo begged.

"No squirrel is a match for me," I told her.

Was I scared? Of course I was.

But I'm going to rule the world. So I had to show *everyone* that I could stand up to anything. Even a terrifying, mean, bullying squirrel.

And I knew I could do it. This was my destiny, after all.

Steve looked nervous, but he rolled open the glass gate. I charged out across the back porch and marched down the steps. I made my way toward Masher.

"Greetings, squirrel," I said. "I am the new ruler of this place. Leave my lawn and never return."

Masher the squirrel looked at me with his mean, shining eyes. He smiled, and the smell of his terrible breath stank even worse than Steve.

"*Your* lawn?" he asked. "This is MY lawn. And no one, especially not a little Chihuahua, is going to make me leave." His voice was raspy. Like nails against a chalkboard. Like sandpaper on metal. Like EVIL.

But I am also evil.

"You are no match for me," I told the terrible squirrel.

"Oh really?" Masher asked. He showed me all of his razor-sharp teeth. "You want to rule this neighborhood? Meet your future subjects!"

And then came the ATTACK.

CHAPTER 5

Acorns, Acorns, Everywhere!

The first acorn pelted my nose. The second hit my ear. I ducked. But a third came at me like a cannonball.

"AAAAAAHH!!" I yelled.

There was no escape!

"How dare you attack me?!" I shouted.

Acorns flew from every direction. The squirrels threw them from the trees, the fence, even the roof!

Masher thumped his giant tail and laughed. "This neighborhood is mine!" he yelled.

Suddenly, I understood why Masher was so powerful.

He wasn't just a mean, bullying squirrel. He led his very own *squirrel army*.

"AWHOOOO!" I howled in anger. I hoped my horrible howl would make Masher quake with fear.

THWACK. Another acorn hit my nose.

I couldn't do anything but run.

"Quickly, new guy!" Steve yelled from the porch door. "Follow the sound of my voice!"

I could barely see through the flying acorns. But I followed Steve's voice. And also, his smell.

"Over here!" Steve yelled.

I was almost there. Then, *BAM*. Another acorn knocked me down.

Then suddenly, the world went dark. A shape blocked out the sun. And a giant voice boomed, "I've got him!"

A HUGE nose pushed me in through the porch door. Steve rolled the door shut behind us. I looked up at my rescuer.

"Hello," boomed the giant.

And then and there, in front of my future subjects and my new squirrel enemies, I fainted.

CHAPTER 6

Big Dog, Little Dog

Dreams swirled around me. I saw a squirrel standing over the world, *my* world. Then a voice spoke through my nightmare.

"Wake up!" it boomed.

"Gah!" I jumped to my paws.

"Good job, Zar!" Steve said. "You brought him back to life!"

I looked up. A GIANT dog grinned down at me.

"I'm Zar," the giant dog boomed. "I'm a Russian wolfhound. I live next door."

"Thank you for rescuing me, Zar," I said. I wanted to impress this new dog. But it was hard, since the army of squirrels was still outside, laughing.

The crowd of squirrels parted, and Masher came through. He grinned.

"You'll pay for this," I said. I tried to sound as evil as possible. But it sounded more like a croak. From a frog with a cold.

"Oooooh, I'm so scared," Masher said. The way he said it meant he was *not* scared. "What could a tiny pet like you ever do to me?" he asked.

My fur stood on end. I couldn't think of anything to say.

Masher laughed one more time. Then he ran off over the fence. His squirrel army followed.

My ears drooped.

"Wow! Masher really got you," Steve said.

"Yes. But this was just our first meeting," I said. I was trying to make myself feel better.

"Are you sure you're okay? He hit you with a lot of acorns," Steve added.

"I'm fine," I said again, but my ears drooped a little more.

"Uh, Steve, maybe let the new guy have some space," Neo said.

"No, I mean, he *really* beat you. You were no match for him. I was worried," Steve went on.

"Steve!" BeBe said.

But my ears were now so low, they were brushing the floor.

"Oh, sorry," Steve said. "I didn't mean to make you sad. You can do it! Go Team New Guy!"

"Thank you, Smelly Steve," I said. I buried my face in my paws. "But you are right. Maybe I was wrong about my destiny."

Zar looked puzzled.

"I am destined to rule this world," I explained. "Or at least, I thought I was."

"Cheer up, new guy," Neo said. "We can show you the good spots in the yard. The squirrels are all gone now."

I looked outside. Neo was right. They were gone, probably off to scare more pets.

Steve rolled the door open. The smells of the yard floated in. It would be so nice to explore.

I stood up. I lifted a paw to take a step out the door.

My paw shook. "I . . . I can't do it," I said. I was too afraid.

And how could I take over the world if I couldn't even go into the backyard?

The other pets tried to cheer me up. But nothing could make me feel better. I lay in the kitchen all afternoon.

Until suddenly, the front door swung open, and Lucy burst in.

"Hello, puppy!" she said. "Who's ready for a name?"

I closed my eyes, awaiting my terrible fate.

CHAPTER 7

A Ruler Reborn

Come with me," Lucy said. She picked me up under one arm, and pointed forward with the other. Mr. Chin, Mrs. Chin, and Kevin followed.

"Good luck, new guy!" Steve squeaked from the bottom of the stairs.

He was excited, but I was nervous. I didn't think this was going to go well.

Lucy brought us into her room. It was decorated with white flowers and posters of animals.

"I got the idea here," she said.

I couldn't look. What if she named me "Tulip" after her flower pillows, or "Butterfly" after her posters?

But then—

Thunk. She was pointing to a giant map on the wall. A map filled with VOLCANOES.

"Sometimes big things, like volcanoes, can change an entire landscape. But sometimes the smallest things are the most powerful. One tiny ember can start a raging forest fire. It's small but mighty. Like him!"

Lucy pointed at me.

"*Ember!*" Mrs. Chin said. "It's the perfect name."

"Ember," I said to myself. I felt hope swirl inside me.

"Human," I barked, "you have done well. I accept this destiny." My tail began to wag.

"He likes it!" Lucy said.

Mrs. Chin clapped, and even Kevin smiled.

"Well, *Ember* it is, I guess," Mr. Chin said.

"Ember the Mighty," Lucy said, holding me up.

"With you at my side, we will rule the world," I told her. I gave her a lick on the ear.

"I love you, too," Lucy said.

Lucy took me for a walk before bed. I stayed close to her. Everywhere I looked, I thought I saw the flash of a squirrel tail. Also, trash cans.

But soon I will rule this kingdom. And then, NONE of these things will be allowed.

That night, while the humans ate dinner, I got back to business. It was time to come up with a plan to defeat Masher the Monster Squirrel. After he was gone, nothing would stand in my way. The world would be mine.

When the Chins went into the living room to watch TV, I raced upstairs to find Neo and Steve.

"I have a plan," I told them. "We go after their acorns!"

"Why?" Neo asked.

"The acorns are the source of the squirrels' power," I said. "So tomorrow, we'll steal them. Without their acorns, the squirrels will have nothing to throw at us. Then Masher will be defeated."

"Wow," Neo said. "That makes sense!"

"Neo, you'll go first to scout ahead and find the acorn stash," I explained. "Then Steve, you'll distract the squirrels. Zar and I will be hiding in the next yard over, and while the squirrels are busy, Neo will lead us to the acorns, and we'll get rid of them."

"But what will we do with all the acorns?" Steve asked. "Even *I* can't eat that much at once."

"Leave that to me and Zar," I said with a grin. "With his size, and my evil genius, *nothing* will stop us."

Neo and Steve thought it was a good plan. How could it not be? It was thought up by me.

Ember the Mighty.

Dark Lord reborn.

CHAPTER 8

Pi-RATS

By the next afternoon, we were ready to attack.

Neo flew high above the neighborhood, searching for the acorn stash. Steve was at the porch door. And Zar and I were in the next yard over, waiting for the signal.

Squirrels were scattered around the lawn. Masher watched them from a high tree branch.

Neo flew in circles, and I worried. What if she never found the stash?

But suddenly, she changed course. She came zooming straight down toward us.

"I found it!" Neo said. "I found the acorns!"

"Excellent!" I said. "Give Steve the signal!"

Neo fluttered to the porch.

"Now, Steve!" she said.

And our plan was set in motion.

"FOR KEVINNNNNNN!!" Steve yelled.

And then, he rolled out. Literally.

My jaw dropped in surprise. Steve was supposed to just run around in the yard, distracting the squirrels. But he'd done something even better. He was in a big, clear *ball*. And he was FAST.

Steve zoomed out faster than a tennis ball, faster than Masher's troops.

"Well done, Steve!" I barked.

"This way!" Neo said, fluttering into the bushes behind the house. I followed. Or really, I commanded, and Zar followed. Because I wasn't on my own. I rode a mighty steed.

A mighty steed named Zar.

I knew I could conquer the yard with a giant Russian wolfhound on my side.

I looked behind me as we galloped after Neo. Steve was spinning in circles around Masher. Masher was thumping his tail and directing his troops to hit Steve with acorns. But the acorns just bounced off the ball.

I knew that victory was at hand.

Neo led us through the woods behind the house. At first, I couldn't see anything but leaves. But then, there it was!

The massive tower of acorns was the squirrels' greatest weapon. Without their acorns, they would be powerless.

Zar filled his huge mouth with acorns.

"Come, Zar! Take as much as you can!" I urged him on.

Zar ran back to the hole we'd dug at the edge of the lawn. He spit the acorns out into the hole. "Next! Faster!" I cried from his back.

I knew this plan couldn't fail. Zar would bury the acorns, and the squirrels would have nothing to throw at us. We would win, and—

"Squeak!" A sound made us both jump.

It was a rat. A guard rat. It was hiding beneath a pile of leaves by the acorn pile.

Zar froze.

"It's just a rat, Zar," I said. "Onward!"

"I'm scared of rats . . ." Zar said, backing up nervously.

"It's tiny," I said. "It's practically a mouse! You could squish it with your paw!"

"Its teeth are like SPIKES," Zar said.

The rat's eyes were wide with fear. It stared at Zar. "Squeak?" the rat said.

"It's scared of *you*!" I said.

"It's going to *eat* me!" Zar said.

The rat took one tiny, nervous step forward.

"CHARGE!" I said.

"Retreat!" Zar said.

And I'm sure you can guess what happened next.

CHAPTER 9

I Capture the Chair

Zar and I raced through the side door just as Steve and Neo came in through the porch. I rolled the porch gate shut.

"Did you see that?" Steve said, smiling and puffing out his fur. "I was so fast! Those squirrels never suspected a thing! And now we have all their acorns."

Zar hid his face in his paws.

"Um, we have their acorns, right?" Steve asked.

"My plan didn't quite work. There were some snags," I said.

"Snags?! We almost DIED," Zar said. "There were rats! Killer pirate rats! I'm scared of rats!" He flung himself on the rug and covered his eyes with his paws.

"Um, Zar," I said. "It was just one rat. And, I know it is a little late to be asking this. But what else are you afraid of?"

"Oh, just mice, spiders, moths, the vacuum, the garbage disposal, the . . ."

Zar went on, but I stopped listening. It was time for a new plan. A new plan that maybe didn't rely on Zar.

"Let's take a rest," I said. "We can regroup in the afternoon."

But even resting had problems.

When Mr. Chin came home and saw the dirt all over my fur, I was *forced* into the sink for a bath. I do not want to say more about this TERRIBLE ordeal.

Once I was dry, I escaped the kitchen. I wanted to climb onto the living room couch to look out over my kingdom. But Mrs. Chin ran in.

"Shoo!" she said. "No dogs on the furniture!"

"Be careful, human," I barked. "When I rule this kingdom, this couch will be mine, too."

But she said, "Shoo!" again, so I leapt down.

It seemed like everyone was against me.

But then—

"Psst," Lucy called. She was curled up in the big armchair doing homework. "Ember, come here." She patted the seat.

I leapt up and licked her ear. She laughed.

"The world will be ours," I woofed. "I can feel it!"

"Good dog," Lucy whispered. "Of course you can come on the furniture—this is your home, too! Just stay on this side of me, so Mom can't see you. Besides, you blend in with the cushion. It works perfectly."

Lucy did her homework, and I lay on the arm of the chair, careful to stay hidden from Mrs. Chin. I could see out the window into the neighborhood. It was a strange, scary land. But I knew it could be something more. It could be *mine*.

I thought about Lucy's words. I was at home here. I blended in.

I sat up with a gasp. THAT WAS IT! I KNEW WHAT TO DO!

CHAPTER 10

Mission Impossi-Bug

I ran upstairs and burst into Mr. and Mrs. Chin's bedroom.

"BeBe, you are the key!" I said, running to the fern by the window. "I need you to go on a top secret spying mission. Are you up for the job?"

"Absolutely!" BeBe said, waving at me from a leaf. "I've always wanted a job!"

"The mission is simple," I said. "Neo will fly you over to the house where Masher lives. She will leave you on the windowsill outside Jimmy's—his human's—room. Get inside and find a place to hide and listen. Neo will fly back and forth to tell us what you hear."

"Sounds fun!" BeBe said.

We waited until the next morning. As soon as everyone left for school and work, we jumped into action.

Neo and BeBe flew toward Jimmy's house. Steve and I waited in Lucy's room.

"You come up with great plans, Ember," Steve said.

"Thank you," I said. "I had a long time to think about world domination in the shelter. That's why I plan to rule the world. That way, NO ONE can ever hold me prisoner again."

"That must have been hard," Steve said.

"It was," I said. "But they couldn't keep me there forever."

"Yeah, luckily," Steve said. "Now you have us! And we have you."

I hadn't really thought about this. Steve was right. My subjects in this kingdom were becoming more like friends. And I didn't know what to say.

"Th-thank you, Smelly Steve," I said finally. "I am honored to be a Chin."

We sat there quietly for a moment.

And then suddenly, we both jumped. A familiar voice was yelling outside the window.

"Help! Help!" Neo chirped. "It's Lucy!"

"What?!" I asked.

"Jimmy saw her walking by his house on her way to school. He took her science books, and he's making fun of her. He's making her *cry*."

"LUCY IS IN DANGER!" I cried.

"Wait, Ember! We need a plan!" Neo called from the windowsill.

But I was already racing down the steps and to the front door. I nudged it open with my nose. I needed to get to Lucy.

"Ember, no!" Steve called from upstairs.

"Wait, bad dog!" Mr. Chin yelled. He came running into the front hall from the kitchen.

He chased me.

But I was too fast for him.

I ran out the door!

I ran down the front steps!

I paused. The sidewalk was scarier than the yard! Who knows what could be out there? But I had to keep going. Lucy needed me!

I dashed down the street and came face-to-face with . . . A TRASH CAN. My hair stood on end. But no, Lucy needed me!

I ran past the trash can.

All around me were terrifying things. I knew that squirrels or strangers or falling trash cans could jump out at me at any moment.

But I could only think of Lucy—and how scared and alone she must feel.

"This way!" Neo called, flying above me. "They're just around the corner!"

Neo led me toward Jimmy's house: where Masher, and other evils, waited for me.

CHAPTER 11

A Spark into a Flame

I turned the corner to Jimmy's street and saw Jimmy and Lucy.

Jimmy was big and scary, just like Masher. He didn't have razor-sharp teeth like Masher, but he might as well have.

Jimmy grinned as he held Lucy's science books above his head.

And Lucy, *my* Lucy, stood there with tears on her face, reaching for her books.

She clearly didn't know what to say, or what to do.

But *I* did.

"YOU GET AWAY FROM HER!" I barked in my meanest, biggest voice. I leapt onto Jimmy's boots, and I didn't care how big or heavy they were. I began to tear at them with my claws. "Fear me! You will regret this day!"

I bit into his shoelaces.

"Aaaaah! Get this dog off of me!" Jimmy yelled, shaking his foot.

But I held on. "YOUR DOOM IS HERE!" I growled. My fur stood on end.

He shook his foot again. I could barely hold on. One more kick, and he was going to fling me into the air.

"LEAVE HIM ALONE!" a BIG voice called out. It was a loud voice. A strong voice. A LUCY VOICE.

"You leave my dog alone, Jimmy." Lucy stepped forward, all her fear gone.

"You leave my dog alone, and you give me back my books. Otherwise, I'll tell your parents and make sure you're grounded for the rest of your life. Understand?" She  pointed her finger right in his face.

Now it was *Jimmy* who looked scared.

Lucy was still Lucy, but she seemed bigger. Her confidence made her grow. Like a spark. Like an ember.

And no one could stand in her way.

"S-s-sorry," Jimmy said in a small voice. He put his foot down. He handed Lucy back her books.

I felt gentle hands pick me up from Jimmy's shoe.

"Let's go, Ember," Lucy said in her new big voice, full of confidence.

We walked home together. Me, Ember, future ruler of this realm. And Lucy, another future leader of this world.

"Next, we'll take on Masher," I barked at Lucy. "And then, after Masher, THE WORLD."

I knew that with Lucy at my side, I could do *anything*.

CHAPTER 12

Type "A" for Animal Control

Bad dog for running away!" Mr. Chin said, after Lucy brought me home and left for school. "But also, good dog for protecting Lucy," Mr. Chin went on. "Very good dog."

For once, I let him scratch my ears. I even rolled over so he could rub my belly.

Maybe these humans were okay after all.

I made my way upstairs. Steve was waiting for me.

"That was AMAZING, Ember!" Steve said. "You saved Lucy!"

"Thank you," I said.

"But also, what will we do about Masher? Jimmy's defeated, but Masher is still out there with his acorns!" Steve said.

"I don't know. But with friends like you by my side, we will win in the end," I said.

Just then, Neo flew in through the open window, with BeBe on her back.

"Hey, guys! Spying is SO MUCH fun!" BeBe said.

"I'm glad you enjoyed it, loyal bug," I said.

"Yeah, and I learned SO MUCH about Masher while Jimmy was outside," BeBe went on, waving her legs excitedly. "He misses the woods! He doesn't like being Jimmy's pet. Did you know the woods have squirrels everywhere? And they spend their days playing? They don't have to bully anyone, because there are acorns EVERYWHERE, so there's plenty to share."

"BEBE!" I cried. "You brilliant spy. You have SAVED us!"

"Oh yay!" BeBe said. "Saved us from what?"

But I was too busy making my plan to answer.

We did not have long to wait. When Mrs. Chin came home, we sprang into action. Neo flew in circles around the house, chirping loudly. While the Chins chased her, Steve and I pulled Mrs. Chin's phone out of her purse.

We hid it under the couch until Mr. and Mrs. Chin went to pick Lucy up from school. They were going to have a talk with the principal about bullying. And then, they were going for ice cream.

Once they were gone, we crowded around Mrs. Chin's phone. It took some tries, but between me and BeBe, with Neo helping with spelling, we sent a text to Animal Control.

An hour later, we gathered in the backyard. We watched as humans dressed in uniforms came into the yard. They carried one very big, very happy squirrel to their van.

I waved my paw, and Masher waved his. We had been enemies. But now we said goodbye. And I was happy for him.

"We won!" Steve said, turning flips on the grass, once the van had gone. "I've never won anything before! We should celebrate! What can we eat?!"

"We won," I said. "Thanks to all of you. You will be rewarded." I smiled at my subjects, my new friends.

Our victory would have been complete there.

But that night, there was one more victory in store.

Because that night, I didn't sleep on my tiny bed in the kitchen.

I slept on a real bed. In a room filled with posters and maps and diagrams of volcanoes.

I was curled up at Lucy's side. Just where I belonged.

As I slept, I dreamed of world domination.

Which would begin the very next day.

CHAPTER 13

Next Stop, the World

The next day, I surveyed the house—my new kingdom.

It was the weekend, which meant all the Chins were home. Steve was rolling around in his ball, and Neo was on her downstairs perch.

I sat on the couch and watched them all. I would rule this place now. Nothing stood in my way.

"Lucy, come to the computer!" Mrs. Chin yelled from the kitchen. "It's Poh Poh!"

"Poh Poh is Lucy's grandma," Neo said.

"Oh yay!" Lucy cried. She ran to the kitchen.

I followed her, curious. Smelly Steve rolled after me, and Neo flew behind.

Poh Poh seemed like a nice, white-haired, older version of Lucy. She smiled and waved from the screen. "Guess what?" she said with a smile. "I'm coming to visit next week!"

"Yay!" Lucy said.

"GASP," Neo and Steve said.

"What's wrong?" I asked.

But before they could answer, a new face appeared on the screen.

It was a gray poodle, with gigantic, evil eyes.

"DOOM," the poodle said.

"That's Poh Poh's dog, Fluffy," Neo whispered. "He always comes when she visits."

"Does he want to rule the world, too?" I asked, worried.

"No," Steve replied in a hushed voice. "He wants to *destroy* it."

Susan Tan lives in Cambridge, Massachusetts. She grew up with lots of small dogs who all could rule the world. Susan is the author of the Cilla Lee-Jenkins series, and *Ghosts, Toast, and Other Hazards*. She enjoys knitting, crocheting, and petting every dog who will let her. Pets Rule! is her first early chapter book series.

Wendy Tan Shiau Wei is a Chinese-Malaysian illustrator based in Kuala Lumpur, Malaysia. Over the last few years, she has contributed to numerous animation productions and advertisements. Now her passion for storytelling has led her down a new path: illustrating children's books. When she's not drawing, Wendy likes to spend time playing with her mix-breed rescue dog, Lucky. The love for her dog is her inspiration to help this book come to life!

Pets RULE!

My Kingdom of Darkness

Questions & Activities

Look-up the definition of the word *minion*. Why does Ember call the humans minions? What does this tell you about his plans for world domination?

Why does Ember dislike the name *Chuckles*? Why does Lucy decide to name him *Ember* instead?

Who are the three other pets who live in the Chin house? How does Ember feel about the other pets?

What is Ember's plan to destroy the acorn stash? Why doesn't the plan work?

Ember calls the Chins' house his *kingdom*. Draw and label a map of the Chins' house, as if *you* were Ember! For instance, what would you call the kitchen, and Lucy's room?

CPSIA information can be obtained
at www.ICGtesting.com
Printed in the USA
BVOW09s2226110917
494598BV00001B/1/P

BIOGRAPHICAL NOTE

Pope Brock is a writer, teacher and DJ living in Arlington, Massachusetts. He is the author of two previous books: *Indiana Gothic* (Doubleday/Nan A. Talese), about the murder of his great-grandfather; and *Charlatan: America's Most Dangerous Huckster, the Man Who Pursued Him, and the Age of Flimflam* (Crown), about the most successful quack in American history. His articles have appeared in *GQ*, *Esquire*, *Rolling Stone*, *London Sunday Times Magazine*, and many other publications. Since 2005 he has taught in the low-residency MFA Writing Program at the University of Nebraska.

PRAISE FOR

POPE BROCK

"Pope Brock is the sky-gazer and writer our culture needs at this moment. This book is deft, funny, profound in its implications—and also a grave prediction about the mess that may soon be transferred from Earth to the moon. A beguiling and original story by a writer whose wisdom is only matched by his wicked comic timing."

—SARAH BRAUNSTEIN, author of *The Sweet Relief of Missing Children*

"Whenever I'm reading a Pope Brock book I always fall for the writing and then for him. This book about the moon is his most deliciously, comically personal one. Though the reader finds herself in happy contemplation of crisping ex-lovers with lasers from a future lunar workplace, or perhaps having imperfect sex in perfect spheres of water, or simply socializing on the moon with well-adapted sociopaths, nevertheless we also get to know the fiercely earthbound heart of Pope Brock. His is a vision both funny and horrifying, a Seussian galaxy of rumpus absurdity and straight-talking hard truths. By the end of it one thinks, 'Ah, Humanity' but right upon that one thinks, 'Thank goodness for Pope Brock.'"

—LEIGH ALLISON WILSON, author of *From the Bottom Up*

ANOTHER FINE MESS

Life on Tomorrow's Moon

Pope Brock

 Red Hen Press | *Pasadena, CA*

Illustrations by John Cote
Book design by Selena Trager

Library of Congress Cataloging-in-Publication Data
Names: Brock, Pope, author.
Title: Another fine mess : life on tomorrow's Moon / Pope Brock.
Description: First edition. | Pasadena, CA : Red Hen Press, [2017]
Identifiers: LCCN 2017011349 | ISBN 9781597090407 (softcover : acid-free
paper) | ISBN 9781597095075 (ebook)
Classification: LCC PS3552.R612 A6 2017 | DDC 814/.54—dc23
LC record available at https://lccn.loc.gov/2017011349
Elements of Chapter 1 appeared originally in *Meridian*

The National Endowment for the Arts, the Los Angeles County Arts Commission, the Dwight Stuart Youth Fund, the Max Factor Family Foundation, the Pasadena Tournament of Roses Foundation, the Pasadena Arts &
Culture Commission and the City of Pasadena Cultural Affairs Division,
the City of Los Angeles Department of Cultural Affairs, the Audrey & Syd-
ney Irmas Charitable Foundation, Sony Pictures Entertainment, Amazon
Literary Partnership, and the Sherwood Foundation partially support Red
Hen Press.

First Edition
Published by Red Hen Press
www.redhen.org

ACKNOWLEDGMENTS

My great thanks to those who have helped me on this strange odyssey which, however slim the results, took me almost as long as the original Greek one. I'm particularly grateful to a number of experts who generously shared their time and thoughts with me: Dr. Bernard Foing, a principal-project lunar scientist with the European Space Agency; Dr. Paul Spudis of the Lunar and Planetary Institute in Houston; Prof. Madhu Thangavelu of the Department of Astronautical Engineering at the University of Southern California; Dr. Patricia Santy, former flight surgeon and psychiatrist at NASA's Johnson Space Center; James Wesley Rawles, former US Intelligence Officer and survival-retreat consultant; Dr. Gioia Massa, "veggie" scientist at the Kennedy Space Center in Florida (thanks to Patricia Henley for the introduction); Hans-Jurgen Rombaut of the Rotterdam Academy of Architecture; Rick Steiner (not the professional wrestler), marine conservation specialist with Oasis Earth; and Prof. Edward Gleason, manager/astronomer of the Southworth Planetarium at the University of Southern Maine.

My gratitude (inadequate word) to the gang at the University of Nebraska's MFA in Writing Program, where I teach, who gave me so much love and help with this project over the long haul, and to my writing group in Maine—Sarah Braunstein, Annie Finch, and Kristin Ghodsee—for their friendship and fantastic advice.

Without the professionals in my corner I probably wouldn't be writing this page at all, especially of course Kate Gale, Mark Cull, and the dedicated crew at Red Hen Press. Thanks also to my agent, David Black of the David Black Literary Agency, for his unshakeable faith in his client, and to Jennifer Herrera for her smarts and skills.

John Cote's inspired illustrations have taken this book to another level—you'll see what I mean—and dogged expert Terry Hill made the other pictures possible (the world of obtaining permissions is grueling, mysterious, and perverse).

Thanx and a tip of the Hatlo hat to my aunt, Mary Jane Brock, who remembered that garden out back as if it were yesterday.

To Maureen Tobin, I wish I had listened to you sooner.

Finally, and most of all, my love and gratitude to Sarah Wright.

For Dillon, the poet voyager, and for Hannah,
who saw the stars in the ceiling

CONTENTS

If dreams were thunder
And lightning was desire
This old house would have burned down
A long time ago.

—John Prine

CHAPTER 1

WHAT IT TAKES

I was slung in my favorite deck chair, drink in hand, having a gawk at the night sky. Andromeda, Pisces . . . I trawled the constellations, mind abandoned, still aware in some curve at the back of my brain that the world is coming apart at the seams and we're all fucked, and enjoying the gentle paradox of it, the clink of the ice in my glass and the slumber of the dog.

By and by I found my gaze resting on the moon. There it was, the great provider: breeder of wonder, werewolves and all those songs. The place where beauty meets philosophy, where hope and despair alike are lost.

Gnawing through the romance though was a little something I'd read not long before. An astrophysicist had claimed that the moon could save our planet. Not immediately: this would be in about 4.5 billion years when the sun explodes and roasts us in wrath and fire unless we get out of the way.

Frankly, the notion of Earth making a break for it seemed implausible to me, but this Canadian professor said we could do it by shooting off an army of rockets on the far side of the moon. Slammed out of its orbit by the collective blast, the moon would sail off with Earth, yoked by gravity, trailing behind it. A thousand years' travel and we're out of harm's way—albeit dark and freezing unless we initiate phase two of the plan. As the sun recedes in the distance, we would replace its rays with a trillion lunar argon arc lamps. A flip of the switch and the moon becomes the sun: blue sky, puffy clouds, everything just as before.

I'm gazing up at the night, not quite in a reverie thanks to the gnats, but thinking yes, well, lovely. Imagine the parades. Still, to get that opportunity the human race would have to last (*long pause, phone math*) 22,500 times longer than it has already. At that point I heaved myself up and went inside for more booze.

Looking back, I believe that night marked the shift in my thinking from save it (Earth) to save us (me). Or if not me, someone. Because when you've got surfing champs riding the curl from an ice wall collapsing in the Arctic, when an Ivy League egghead offers mathematical proofs that the human race is doomed if we don't get off-world, and Stephen Hawking and others are ululating on the same theme, and thousands are tunneling and stockpiling ahead of TEOTWAWKI (The End of the World as We Know It), then you have to start

wondering if it's not time to break camp. Or at least to establish a beachhead on the moon, just as some governments,
corporations, scrappy start-ups and freestanding oddballs
are trying now to do.

Granted, we've heard such talk before, back in the days of
the Apollo program. Lunar colonies they promised us, farms,
industries, a platform to the universe. What did we get? June
2008: "Space Station Resident Fixes Toilet." The big difference
today is that some people are actually serious about it. In the
60s it was just something to say. For despite all the soaring
rhetoric the only thing Washington really cared about then
was beating the Soviets there.

As a kid when I heard the word *Soviets*, I got a taste in my
mouth like lead pencils. I remember a *Weekly Reader* from
maybe fourth grade with a picture of J. Edgar Hoover beneath the headline, "What You Can Do in the Fight Against
Communism." What winning would mean—*Let's Win the
Cold War!*—no one ever explained, but the consequences of
losing were clear. The Kremlin and the Kingston Trio agreed,
when the big one hit, we'd all go, next year, next month, tomorrow . . . Everyone lived in a state of controlled hysteria
and doublethink. To safeguard the nation the Atomic Energy
Commission put out a call to any and all Americans to get out
there and find more uranium so the government could build
more bombs. *We pay cash!* People were streaming across the
Colorado Plateau with picks and shovels, Geiger counters,

whole families, some in the newly popular uranium designer-wear including the form-fitting "U-235 suit" for Mom and the "Digerette Jr." model for Sis. No protection from radiation expressed or implied but so what? Handling uranium was safe. People believed this not just because the Mouseketeers were out looking for it, or even because the government said it was safe. *They believed it because it was impossible.* A lot of these same folks were putting fallout shelters in their homes. Everybody was. My parents got one immediately. We had a small basement and the shelter took up half of it: a little blockhouse of dank concrete with cans and shelving. My mother had to squeeze past it to get to the dryer. Even as a child I knew that sealing the five of us up together for more than an hour and a half was inconceivable on its face. I'd returned home from the dentist one day to find our cat had killed our hamsters and our dog had killed our cat. That was the kind of vibe our house produced among pets in the living room. Put the people in a hole and you can imagine.

Then Sputnik went up. This was in the fall of 1957, and the whole country plotzed. I remember standing in the backyard on those autumn evenings, like millions of other Americans, staring dumbly at the sky trying to spot its winking light. Every ninety minutes the thing passed overhead, accidentally opening and closing garage doors, and with each orbit the Soviets claimed the universe one more time.

What would the Commies do next? Would they bomb us from outer space? *Would they bomb us from the moon?*

Not to worry, the Russians said. True, in five to ten years they would be enthroned there but strictly in the interests of peace and science. At eight I was merely skeptical. Washington's response recalled the time the great acting teacher Stella Adler told her students to react to the bombing of Pearl Harbor as if they were chickens. One of the first ideas advanced, perhaps predictably, was to nuke the moon.

To be fair, it wasn't the only thing American officials wanted to nuke. If there was one group in those days even more in thrall to the bomb than everyone else, it was the people in charge of it, many of whom united the self-surrender of cultists with a sort of mad curiosity about what it could do. The Atomic Energy Commission went on a campaign to create a deep-water harbor in Alaska with five thermonuclear bombs. But the moon! Not only could we keep the Russians at bay by firing a warning shot into its head; the demonstration of strength would have "beneficial psychological results" for our citizens, as Jet Propulsion Lab chief J. H. Pickering explained—plus, he said, scientists could harvest and study the hail of radioactive debris. Thus in 1958, top-secret Project A119 got the go-ahead with prestige support from the RAND Corporation and JPL. A modest strike, the planners said. We won't be obliterating the whole moon any more than we destroyed all Japan.

Ten months of work was sunk in this scheme. Along the way team member Carl Sagan, later the face of space on public television, established that a Hiroshima-sized blast in lunar gravity would fly in all directions, not mushroom as on Earth, a plus propaganda-wise since it would be easier to see.

Then just like that it was over. NASA was born and the project was scrapped. The new, karmically improved plan was to put men on the moon before the Russians could. For a time this looked unlikely. The Soviets orbited the first animals, the first man, two men, three, the first woman, with a vaudevillian's arrogant skill, while NASA's small successes splashed down to a mix of scorn and anxious clapping. But derailed by infighting, the Russians flagged, and on July 20, 1969, there was Apollo 11 touching down and America waving the big foam finger.

Ironically, when TV screens showed that white beetle climbing down the ladder, it didn't matter who had won. That's what people said, and for a moment it was true.

We're on our way! NASA cried. Next stop the stars!

But with the Russians beaten the rest was gravy, or would have been except there was no gravy: up close the moon seemed to have nothing a person would actually want. By the mid-1970s NASA's budget had dropped dramatically, and as an icon of the age the moon faded out, to be replaced by the disco ball in *Saturday Night Fever*.

Why then, all these decades later, the hunger to return to the big white stone? What's driving it? The one-world ethos of the Apollo program is long gone. Humanity in the main couldn't care less about understanding the cosmos. Saving mankind? You couldn't get the funding.

We're going back because, like the voice of Gatsby's beloved Daisy, the moon is full of money.

In the 1990s the rumors began: talk of new fuels there, strange isotopes. Probes from India, China, the US dove and hovered like hornets over a jam pot. Then water! Confirmed! In two shakes the moon went from a circular corpse to a whiteboard covered in calculations. Ever since masses of helium were found there, an isotope rare on Earth, some have been calling the moon the "Persian Gulf of the 21st century." Others foresee there the industrial hub of the inner solar system. They see alien-hunting telescope farms, hotels, zoos, gardens, and everyone having sloooooow sex in 1/6th Earth's gravity. Plus swimmers like flying fish, cubic basketball, gymnasts like figures in a dream. Lunar eveningwear! Genetic warehousing! Glass roads!

Not everyone is thrilled at the prospect. Among those filled with loathing and dismay are Navahos, Hindus, practicing witches and legions of secularists for whom the moon represents religion's last dim chime. Eco-activist Rick Steiner of Alaska has petitioned the United Nations to have the moon declared a World Heritage Site on the theory that man,

having made a latrine of Earth, will do the same to the moon only faster.

The nobility of that impulse, I have to say, struck me a few beats late. When I first heard talk of "malling the moon," my thoughts jumped to: here come people with lots of money about to do things to make lots more money none of which I will ever get. I want to be upfront about this, how my own forlorn relationship to other people's wealth is part and parcel of my animus against the ultra-rich. I fully believe that much of the misery in this fine pretty world is caused by the privileged class enjoying its obscene privileges. But the rest of my grievance derives from the grinding injustice to me personally. *Where's mine?* So much money in the world and none touches me. It's like the miracle of the Red Sea.

Of course top players in the space business are necessarily loaded. They have daring and pantechnicons of ideas, of which we have already seen early fruits. I've no doubt that when it comes to the moon, these innovators will make many dazzling additions to the catalogue of human ingenuity.

Historically, it's true, our ingenuity has been something of a mixed bag. One might even call it the double helix of enterprise and stupidity that dooms us whenever we get near tools. I think in this regard of Thomas Midgley. He was working as a chemist for General Motors in the 1920s when he realized he could eliminate engine knock by adding tetra-ethyl-lead to gasoline. This was great for car sales, but the stuff was tricky

to produce. Workers handling the new formula suffered lead poisoning so severe it caused nerve damage and wild hallucinations. At the Deepwater, New Jersey, factory they were beating off clouds of imaginary insects. The problem did get straightened out. Not medically, but politically it was totally taken care of. Lead goes up; life goes on. But Midgley's not done. He turns around and invents Freon, first of the fluorocarbons. So now he's the father of ozone-eating coolants too. Later he contracted polio. In 1944 he was struggling with some rigging he'd invented to pull himself out of bed and got tangled in it and accidentally strangled to death, a symbolic gesture if there ever was one.

What's to be done with such a man? Well, put him on the moon and he'd be no threat at all because the moon has no atmosphere. It's idiot-proof in that regard. This is what makes the moon ideal for so many kinds of work. It may be a land of boiling, freezing, radiation and chalk, but our genius can fly free there without opprobrium and reprisals. And a lucky thing too if we have to shift operations in any big way.

We're so busy, all us little Midgleys, that it may just be a question of what triggers the diaspora. Oil? According to one group of catastrophists we'll be ruined suddenly and soon by "peak oil," the term of art for running out of it. But other things could go, *snap*, like that. Peak water, peak farmland, peak fish: pick your death blow. Peak bees! *Where the bee sucks there suck I but now I suck alone.* You've heard of course

about bees disappearing. Perhaps you thought, as I did, of a fuzzy few creeping around on the roses. Not so. We're talking great slabs of bees vanishing wholesale. In California the owner of a commercial apiary lost two billion bees in two weeks. Colony Collapse Disorder: it's happening all over the world. Pretty soon fruits, vegetables, *pfffft*. What's causing it? Everybody's got a theory: Varroa mites, genetically modified crops, cell phone radiation, hillbilly breeding techniques . . . No one's sure. But that's not the weird part. What's weird is their mode of departure. Because they are literally disappearing. It's not as though that guy in California were suddenly shuffling through 40 tons of dead bees, or his neighbor came over and said, "Hey, get your fucking dead bees off my land." There were no corpses found or reported. The bees were just gone. It's as if we've somehow stumbled upon a brand-new recipe, a witches' brew so potent it doesn't just kill things; it makes them actually dematerialize. But since we don't know the formula, all we can do is watch its effects. Where will it strike next? One day we'll step out the door and the dogs or the wheat won't be there. And so it'll go, one thing at a time, until finally people start to vanish and that's when the panic starts. Now crowds are pouring through the streets, trampling others on the run from dirty-bomb threats, London fogs of CO_2, eructations of methane, rogue viruses, not to mention shortages of food, water, Xanax, whatever it is singly or in combination that sends people streaming toward—

toward what? Nobody knows—men, women, children, even the elderly who thanks to medical breakthroughs have joined the growing army of the dead who won't lie down . . .

But to return to first principles: corporations, hand-in-glove with governments, will hegemonize the moon. Broad-brush, that's the plan. Thereafter, whether Earth somehow escapes immolation and becomes the moon's robust trading partner, or turns into a global hospice with thousands of acres of methane rising from ancient graves and the seas so full of jellyfish they look like cobblestones, the human race endures. I'm not promoting here the rancid mythology that business success drives the public good. Rather, I think the process will probably resemble the tale of the scorpion and the frog. Suffering humanity (frog) hitches a ride on the back of the scorpion, hoping against hope that the scorpion will overmaster its own instincts and save them both—which, given the stakes, it may or may not do.

What follows in these pages then is a tour of the grand bazaar, what the place will look like when the Man in the Moon is no longer the sole tenant—*if current plans succeed*. We humans are good at predicting some things, but the future isn't one of them, and here it's a tarot deck with everything wild. All we know for sure is that eager thousands are straining to realize these dreams as we speak.

So with that, let's shed 5/6ths of our body weight and make the leap.

CHAPTER 1 NOTES

[Links live as of this writing]

2   **puffy clouds, everything just as before:** Dr. Leonard White-
head, *Discover Magazine* (July 1996).

surfing champs riding the curl: Watch it happen! "Glacier
Surfing Alaska": https://www.youtube.com/watch?v=mKRR
9RMmcIQ

mathematical proofs that the human race is doomed:
J. Richard Gott III, "Implications of the Copernican Principle for Our Future Prospects," *Nature* 363 (1993). Also: J.
Richard Gott III, "A Grim Reckoning," *New Scientist* (November 15, 1997).

ululating on the same theme: Daniel Cressey, "Get us off
this planet, says Hawking," *Nature News Blog* (April 22,
2008).

stockpiling ahead of TEOTWAWKI: See, e.g., M.D. Creek-
more, "How to Survive TEOTWAWKI in 14 Easy Steps,"
(March 6, 2013), www.thesurvivalistblog.net

3   **Space Station Resident Fixes Toilet:** Juan A. Lozano, *Associated Press* (June 4, 2008).

the Kingston Trio agreed: In a song written by Tom Leh-
rer, "Merry Minuet": https://www.youtube.com/watch?v=
bp6dsKleGpU

4   **"Digerette Jr." model for Sis:** For a full line of uranium-craze
products see: "Collection of Radiation Advertisements from
1940–1960": http://national-radiation-instrument-catalog.com

people in a hole and you can imagine: With luck deranged
neighbors would have torn it down. See "The Shelter," *The
Twilight Zone*, episode 68 (September 29, 1961).

trying to spot its winking light: Contrary to popular belief
there was no winking light.

accidentally opening and closing garage doors: Paul Dickson, *Sputnik: The Shock of the Century* (Walker & Co., 2011).

5   **peace and science:** Albert Parry, "Soviet Cities on the Moon?" *Science Digest* (February 1958).

react to the bombing of Pearl Harbor as if they were chickens: Elaine Stritch, author interview. Marlon Brando laid an egg.

with five thermonuclear bombs: The plan, dubbed Operation Chariot, was championed by Edward Teller, "the father of the hydrogen bomb." For more see Dan O'Neill, *The Firecracker Boys* (Basic Books, 2007).

beneficial psychological results: Gerard Degroot, *Dark Side of the Moon* (NYU Press, 2006).

6   **a plus propaganda-wise since it would be easier to see:** The existence of Project A119 came to light in the 1990s when a biographer of Sagan discovered a reference to it among his papers. Edward Teller wanted to bomb the moon too.

first man, two men, three: "This Day in History, April 12, 1961," http://www.history.com/this-day-in-history/first-man-in-space.

NASA's budget had dropped dramatically: See, e.g., "Office of Management and Budget Historical Tables," *NASA Augustine Spaceflight Review*, Orion (2015).

replaced by the disco ball in *Saturday Night Fever*: It's as great as you remember: "Night Fever Dance—Saturday Night Fever": http://www.youtube.com/watch?v=DhDiWkdnMbQ

7   **full of money:** F. Scott Fitzgerald, *The Great Gatsby* (Scribner, 1925): Chapter 7.

Then water! Confirmed!: Dan Vergano, "NASA: Lunar Water in Crater Confirmed," *USA Today* (October 21, 2010).

the "Persian Gulf of the 21st century": Lawrence E. Joseph, "Who Will Mine the Moon?," *New York Times* (January 19, 1995); Robert Quigley, "Does the Moon Have Military Value?" (January 26, 2016), http://www.themarysue.com

industrial hub of the inner solar system: Adrian Berry, *The Next 500 Years: Life in the Coming Millennium* (W. H. Freeman & Co., 1996).

8   **Thomas Midgley:** Celebrated in various dark corners of the Internet as well as in print. See, e.g., "Thomas Midgley and the Law of Unintended Consequences," *American Heritage* (Spring 2002). At a gathering of members of the American Chemical Society he demonstrated the safety of chlorofluorocarbons (CFCs) by inhaling the gas and putting a lit candle in his mouth. Late breaking: in a move of unprecedented scope 170 countries agreed to ban the use of fluorocarbons in October 2016.

9   **fly free there without opprobrium and reprisals:** The financial sector was first to understand this. In 1984 Stanley E. Adams, then president of the Lamar Savings and Loan Association, applied to the Texas banking commission for a permit to open a branch office on the moon. Apparently he planned to run this outpost himself since after that his firm was seized by the Federal Home Loan Bank and Adams himself indicted on fourteen counts of fraud. His timing was off, but his instincts were impeccable. Yes, some might dismiss him as a microbe, one germ in the sluice pipes of international finance, but take it to the other extreme. Consider a Wall Street tycoon, a real fat cat. Think of all the things he has to put up with, the token investigations, the crappy publicity. After a while the moon's going to look pretty good. No more face-offs with shareholders, no more ritual hand jobs on Capitol Hill. Of course the titans of today won't have this option. They'll die rich, have their wives and servants killed and buried with them, and that'll be that. But for those coming after, if you've got the resources, who's going to stop you? It's like moving the Colts to Indianapolis; you just load up and go.

peak oil: defined as the moment when the rate of production maxes out, then goes downhill forever. According to Kenneth Deffeyes, professor emeritus at Princeton, the US hit

peak oil in 1971. See his essay "When Oil Peaked" at: http://www.princeton.edu/hubbert/the-peak.html

Peak bees!: Perhaps most sharply evoked in documentaries like *The Vanishing of the Bees* (2009) and *The Strange Disappearance of the Bees* (2011). Not everyone thinks it's so mysterious. See, e.g., Natalia Sanchez, "Monsanto's Pesticides Are Partly Responsible for the Collapse of the Bee" (March 4, 2014), http://guardianlv.com/2014/03/monsantos-pesticides-are-partly-responsible-for-the-collapse-of-the-bee

10   **two billion bees in two weeks:** "Why Have Our Bees Buzzed Off?," *The Sun* (UK) (March 10, 2009).

11   **so full of jellyfish:** To those stranded on Earth the rise in "gelatinous animals" due to spiking temperatures may be of less concern than the appearance of giant rodents. See Lacey Johnson, "Warmer Planet Could Be Dominated by Mosquitoes, Ticks, Rodents and Jellyfish," *Scientific American* (February 20, 2012).

CHAPTER 2

THE TARGET

Once it was filled with juju and mojo. It beamed us messages. It enforced its will. Long gone, those days: now the moon seems to move in a sort of lovely mineral trance. Of course, although we're not its slaves anymore, the spiritual aesthetics of it command us still. We recognize the hold it has on us. At least we think we do. In fact we were right the first time.

The moon teems with power, immense and ungovernable. How immense? There's a cartoon you may know called *Duck Amuck* in which an unseen hand puts Daffy Duck through outrageous changes for almost six minutes. It costumes him a dozen ways, draws different environments around him, covers him in polka dots and erases him a couple of times. That's us in the polka dots. That's the level of magic the moon actually wields. The fact is, without the moon we wouldn't be here at all.

No, not true. Creatures would exist, possibly us. But we wouldn't eat or think the same way, and we'd look completely different.

The moon, you see, holds Earth's axis steady at an angle of roughly 23 degrees. Remove it and our planet would be jumping like a beach ball in a fountain. What's more, instead of revolving at a relatively sedate 1,000 miles an hour, it would be spinning at least three times faster. Under those conditions any activity, from raking the leaves to running a marathon to sitting on a porch swing with your sweetheart on a Saturday night would have to factor in screaming winds and torrential debris spiking into hurricanes above 200 miles an hour. Also, Earth's magnetic field would triple. A magnetic field is good to have because it repels radiation from space. Ramp it up though and asteroids and space junk would be whistling down on us like anvils. Not to mention what it would do to dogs.

I've got a lab mix named Luther. Like most dogs, Luther usually turns and turns before taking a dump. I'd never thought much about it before; it's just one of those things you see. Then I came upon a study published in *Frontiers in Zoology* where I learned that when Luther revolves like that, he is aligning his brain along the north-south axis of Earth's magnetic field. The source of this canine ritual isn't clear, but you can bet that if that force field got a whacking great boost, dogs would know it. What would happen then? Does this mean that outdoors in the usual gale yours would turn three

times faster? Nobody's sure, but you wouldn't notice anyway hanging onto a tree like a flag.

Animal life generally would be much less diverse. Conditions would favor the low, the wide, the vast, the clawed. Plant life would be tough and arthritic.

Given all that, you might think human beings would be toast. Not so. According to Dr. Neil Comins, a physicist who has modeled a moonless Earth, we'd be doing just fine. With our heavy muscles and nose-shield cartilage we would fight and mate at hyper-speed while the sun shot across the sky. Our horse-like ears would turn like radar scanning for news in the din. Speech would be replaced by something else: signaling perhaps, with "moveable appendages" operating as "biological semaphore flags." At night, he says, we might shift to streaming beams of light, a sign language using different colors and intensities. Either that or telepathy.

There's a charged word: telepathy. A sci-fi word. It suggests that thoughts we communicate that way—telepathically— would be smarter than our regular thoughts. They wouldn't be, of course, especially on a moonless Earth where a lot of the messages would be, "Fuck this wind." Which is to say, I believe human nature, which even at its sunniest and most loving is racing little inner highways of secrecy and self-interest, would be even more degraded there. Maybe you feel differently. Maybe you would have preferred rotating ears and a language of lights to what you're lumbered with now.

It's out of our hands either way. Like the Doubtful Guest, the moon isn't going anywhere.

Why is it there at all, you ask?

Well, according to Philippine legend, the moon began as a gleaming silver comb lost in a rice field. The Bomitaba of Africa believed there were once two rival suns, one of which tricked the other into jumping into a pond. Some astronomers today subscribe to the so-called Big Whack theory, which holds that an object bigger than Mars slammed into Earth and exploded, after which some of the debris coalesced into the moon. The Aztecs thought a crazy god chopped off the head of his sister Coyolxauhqui and threw it into the sky. Anything's possible. On one thing today there's general agreement: when it first appeared, the moon was fantastically close, perhaps 15,000 miles out. Imagine it waxing and waning then, how that would have played with your mind. Luckily by the time humans arrived it had retired to its present post a quarter million miles away. And still! Still it ruled our hunts and harvests while we slaughtered our young to appease it.

Someone might be doing the same tonight. Or not. It doesn't matter. The point is that with no moon there would be a different face on the cover of *Vogue*. It owns us even now.

Welcome then to the all-you-can-eat irony that we're planning to own it.

We've seen gestures of the type before. At the Pottsdam Conference in 1945, for example, a surprisingly whimsical Stalin suggested to Roosevelt and Churchill that they carve control of the moon into thirds. But the assault upon it that's gathering now, the genesis of it, lies in the following sequence of events:

In 1967 the United Nations' Outer Space Treaty declared the universe and everything in it "the common heritage of man." One hundred twenty-five countries signed this majestic document.

In 1979 the United Nations' Moon Treaty, specifically tailored, identically framed, was laid before the assembly. This time Kazakhstan and Uruguay signed and almost nobody else. What had happened in the years between was the Apollo program, whose success resonated like the opening bell on Wall Street. There was still no proof the moon held anything more than a bunch of stupid rocks, but a sort of avarice *in potentia* swept the hall: *Sure, it looks worthless, but you never know.*

So now that it looks anything but worthless, various entities are plotting to invade. What should we expect to see when they do? If anything in this life is certain, if history has taught us anything, it's that competitors never vie for treasure on new ground without beating each other's brains out. At least up to now. This time might be different. It's possible that colonizing the moon could proceed in relative tranquility, at least for a good long while.

The first reason you've probably thought of yourself. Breathing is the great leveler. The more time and attention that has to be devoted to ensuring it, the less chance there is of someone launching an attack. But something else too could help keep the peace. It's a humble thought of my own, which I offer for what it's worth.

It has to do with the introduction of laws. Historically, after the first crunch of settlement, they always get passed: first a few, then a lot. Many people ignore or subvert them, but as they proliferate their very existence causes increasing amounts of strife.

On the moon I'd suggest we take a different route and abandon laws altogether.

Let me say right off that I have great respect for the law. Bit by bit, piece by piece down the generations, thousands of extraordinary minds have contributed to make our justice system what it is today, an instrument of great size and complexity affording imaginary protection to the weak. But would we really want to drag the whole can-clanking apparatus all the way to the moon? Where would you put it? On top of which you've got other countries showing up waving their own laws . . .

The most elegant solution in that case would be to toss them all and surrender to the gentle hand of natural law. After all, on the moon it will be extraordinarily hard to commit any "crime" that has to go quickly. You can't run fast or far.

You can't live off the land. Add to that the relative smallness of the population and the wealth of surveillance—imagine how sophisticated then!—and you've got the outlines of a stable society.

In any case, even if civilization on the moon is humming along like a self-regulating watch, there is one keystone of order even life there will demand: the allocation of land. By what mechanism can we establish property rights on the moon?

Given my own bleak history with real estate, and ownership in general, this is a difficult subject for me to take up.

It's a big word, *ownership*, perhaps the most capacious in our language. No other I can think of encompasses such a wide range of experiences. Mine have tended to huddle in one corner of it, which is to say, I've been fucked on every house I ever bought. I was crossing a parking lot once with my real-estate attorney—my in quotes—and the next thing I knew I was signing a revised contract on the hood of a car. When it comes to incurring major obligations, I have a history of indefensible stupidity, and while I no longer sign anything outdoors that's about the only lesson I'm sure I've learned.

But why is this relevant? Why expose my personal failings here? In order to contrast those bummers with the feeling I had buying acreage on the moon.

It cheered me immensely to discover the gossamer world of lunar real estate. For it seems that while actual companies with real equipment are gearing up to tackle the moon,

there's a shadow industry of long standing already selling off lots. The Prospero of this enchanted realm is Dennis Hope of Rio Vista, California. A former shoe salesman and ventriloquist, now "Head Cheese" of the Lunar Embassy, Hope according to press reports has earned millions since 1980 selling off sections of the moon, at first from his house, later through a string of franchises from England to Singapore. Inflamed by his example, other brokers—the Lunar Federation, the Lunar Settlement Initiative, the Luna Society, Lunar Republic Society, Universal Lunarian Society, Lunar Registry ("Don't be fooled by novelty 'lunar property' outfits!") and Artemis—have announced similar offerings.

If you were to ask Mr. Hope how he is able to sell a deed to an acre of the moon for $29.99 + $10.42 shipping and handling, he would tell you that he long ago spied the loophole in the original UN Outer Space Treaty that prohibits nations from claiming title to anything off-Earth, the loophole being that it says nothing about individuals doing it. But that's not the real reason. He can do it because we're allowed by law to be that stupid. No legislature has ever interfered with him, any more than they've banned the selling of magic beans.

So I bought an acre online. Almost instantly three pieces of paper arrived rattling around in a rather large box: the deed itself, a map of the area and a receipt. They weren't fancy. The deed and the map were photocopies. Slurp! Forty bucks was gone.

And yet I felt a strange lightness of heart. In the words of Eli Wallach, "If God did not want them sheared, he would not have made them sheep." I said it to myself, but I felt a breath of healing all the same.

Nevertheless, while Hope and the others have been tootling along for years unmolested, that may change. As settling the moon creeps closer, some legal theorists are getting edgy. Who knows why people buy lunar lots? They can't all be gag gifts. There must be a giant nut factor. What the academics fear, in short, is that once lunar settlements start, waves of these deed-holders will be motoring in from the exurbs of reality to clog the lower courts.

But I have drifted from our original puzzle: how to systematize the non-imaginary distribution of lunar land. OK, here's one proposal. Given that the moon hangs over Earth between latitudes 29 degrees north to 29 south, and given the doctrine of air rights dating back to medieval Roman law (*"For whoever owns the soil, it is theirs up to Heaven and down to Hell"*), a concept ratified by 13th-century glossator Accursius and later enshrined in common law by William Blackstone in his *Commentaries on the Laws of England* (1776), then the moon belongs to Costa Rica, Fiji, Netherlands Antilles, Guatemala and Guam, and together they should control its development.

Failing agreement there, just one path to lunar property remains, namely seizing it, which is where we began. But this

still needn't bring on the usual bloodbath if the method of seizing is telepossession.

Telepossession means staking claims with robots. The idea was born in a storm off the coast of South Carolina in 1857 when the steamer *Central America* sank. Into the vortex went hundreds of passengers and, of more lasting interest, three tons of gold. In the 1980s treasure hunters located the wreck and sent a robot named Nemo down to take pictures and fondle the ingots. The owners of the robot then claimed ownership of the find and (many lawsuits later) prevailed.

Will this principle make telepossession "legal" in space? Of course not, but most in the moon business see it as the logical way to go. By digging trenches, shifting pylons and creeping about with cameras and drills, Earth-guided robots will likely lay title to the first of those unclaimed 9 billion acres. That doesn't mean there won't be problems. I don't see anything to prevent one Earth-guided robot from cruising up behind another and clubbing it to pieces or a Chinese robot locating where Armstrong put that flag and pulling it like a weed. But it's a start. As I mentioned, there are those who fiercely object to sending any spores of plutocracy into space. Moderates are proposing that at least some portions of the moon be set aside Yosemite-style, and perhaps they will. Ultimately though it's hard to see how the preservationist lobby could be anything but road kill on the highway to the stars.

"You can argue the ethics of moon exploitation," writes astronomer Paul Spudis, "but it's inevitable."

Credit: John Cote

And so it has begun, however haltingly, like the first plops in advance of a strong rain. TransOrbital ("The moon is open for business!") received State Department clearance to crash-land customers' poems and phone numbers there, then apparently flatlined. But elsewhere we've seen glimmers of success. The Greeks and Hindus, among other ancient cultures, viewed the moon as a repository for the souls of the dead. So too in its way does Celestis, based in Houston, the first company to fire cremains into the lunar surface.

Celestis has built its business step by step. In 1997 it lofted partial cremains of *Star Trek* creator Gene Roddenberry into

Earth's orbit, along with a quarter ounce of LSD guru Timothy Leary. Having slung the ashes of dozens of others into the void as well—accompanied by huzzahs like "The force be with you" and the more ambiguous "This is for you, Mom!"—Celestis has lately been offering final repose on the moon in several configurations (e.g., two customers blended, $29,995).

Hopeful, that. But before we go any further we should pause to acknowledge that exploiting the moon will entail the displacement of indigenous peoples. That they are fictional has nothing to do with their brilliant variety or the hold they have had on our minds. A tip of the hat then to the blue unicorns, insect men and 6-foot chickens who got there first. Even now it's hard to believe some of those creatures weren't real. In 1638 the Bishop of Hereford wrote of a race of Lunars, tall and radiant beings, living in harmony thanks to a rigorous system of eugenics. Defective Lunars with criminal instincts were put in spaceships and dumped in North America. If they then interbred with the Puritans, think how much that explains.

CHAPTER 2 NOTES

17   *Duck Amuck*: Six well-spent minutes from 1953: Here's
      a sample: https://www.youtube.com/watch?v=nAA3DC
      EkVHs

18   **roughly 23 degrees:** Lisa Grossman, "Many Exo-Earths
      May Have Exo-Moons," *Wired* (June 9, 2011).
      hurricanes above 200 miles an hour: Neil Comins, *What
      If the Moon Didn't Exist?* (HarperCollins, 1993). As he
      notes, this would also be bad for birds.
      he is aligning his brain: Hynek Burda et al., "Dogs are
      sensitive to small variations of the Earth's magnetic field,"
      Frontiers in Zoology (December 27, 2013).

19   **Either that or telepathy:** Neil Comins, op. cit.

20   **Anything's possible:** See, e.g., Jules Cashford, *The Moon:
      Myth and Image* (Basic Books, 2003). For an animated
      rendering of the Big Whack theory see: http://www.pbs
      .org/wgbh/nova/tothemoon/origins2.html

21   **control of the moon into thirds:** Casey Kazan, "The
      Moon & Helium 3—Earth's Energy Salvation," *Daily Gal-
      axy* (February 8, 2007).
      signed this majestic document: Paul Robinson, *Dictio-
      nary of International Security* (Polity, 2008).
      Kazakhstan and Uruguay signed: Edythe Weeks,
      "What's Wrong With the Moon Treaty?," *The Examiner*
      (January 21, 2011).

22   **waving their own laws:** To solve this problem the World
      Space Bar Association of Denver, Colorado has proposed
      a high court modeled on The Hague with a budget "not to
      exceed one quadrillion space dollars." Buzz Aldrin is on
      the board.

23　**the wealth of surveillance:** Whether a life that examined is worth living is a question beyond our scope.

　the outlines of a stable society: Of course no one is ever completely safe:

　signing a revised contract on the hood of a car: Fall 2005.

24　**"Head Cheese" of the Lunar Embassy:** Sources include Robert Roy Britt, "Could Lunar Real Estate Spark a Future War?," *NBC* (February 2, 2004) and Vivian Giang, "The Man Who 'Owns' the Moon Says His Galactic Government Could Solve the Federal Deficit," *Business Insider* (March 19, 2013). If you're looking to purchase: lunarembassy.com. If you'd like to buy a piece of a planet instead: buyuranus.com.

25　**legal theorists are getting edgy:** See, for example, Alan Wasser and Douglas Jobes, "Space Settlements, Property

Rights and International Law," *Journal of Air and Law Commerce* 73, no. 1 (May 5, 2008).

together they should control its development: This concept derives from Robert Heinlein's 1950 science-fiction classic, *The Man Who Sold the Moon*.

26 **(many lawsuits later) prevailed:** "Feds Chase Treasure Hunter Turned Fugitive," *Associated Press* (September 13, 2014). After Thompson won in 1996, things got strange. By 2005 his investors had still received nothing, while Thompson himself was living in semi-squalor in Vero Beach, Florida, and paying his landlord in moldy hundred-dollar bills. Yet he had reportedly stashed at least $2 million in gold coins, among other assets. In 2012 he disappeared leaving behind bank wraps for $10,000 bills and a book entitled *How to Live Your Life Invisible*. He was apprehended, still in Florida, in 2015.

27 **the ethics of moon exploitation:** Paul Spudis, *The Once and Future Moon* (Smithsonian Institution Press, 1996).

The moon is open for business!: Richard Stenger, "Private moon venture given US clearance," *CNN* (September 18, 2002).

cremains into the lunar surface: Beginning with renowned planetary geologist Dr. Eugene Shoemaker in 1998.

28 **LSD guru Timothy Leary:** Marlise Simons, "A Final Turn-On Lifts Timothy Leary Off," *New York Times* (April 22, 1997).

This is for you, Mom!: http://www.celestis.com/memorial/adastra/default.asp

6-foot chickens: Capt. Samuel Brunt, *A Voyage to Cacklogallinia* (1727). The chickens are intelligent but rowdy. "Another diversion they have is making the ostriches run races. The feeding, training and betting on these birds have ruined many of the noblest families. They are also mightily addicted to dice, and will bet and lose their wives

and children, which they sometimes see eaten by the winner, if he is of quality."

race of Lunars: Francis Godwin, *The Man in the Moone: or a Discourse of a Voyage Thither* (1638). Often called the first science-fiction novel in English.

CHAPTER 3

THE TRIP

Customers in space! The time is ripe, the field clear—not counting the International Space Station, a weary fixture that conjures images of, well, nothing, unless it's that shot of Thelma and Louise's car frozen over the gorge. So the spotlight has turned to the private sector, to an ambitious few straining to reclaim space in the name of the people. They themselves are not the people. They are titans of commerce like Richard Branson of Virgin Galactic, Elon Musk of SpaceX, and Jeff Bezos of Amazon. And why not? If we had ever stood onstage swinging Kate Moss in our arms till she nearly came out of her dress (Branson), if Robert Downey Jr. had ever used us as a model for Iron Man (Musk), if we, like Bezos, simply groaned to consume, what would be left to us? Where else to reach but up? With a few smaller companies frisking at the margins, there hasn't been such a sense of wild possibility since 1638

when the Bishop of Hereford sent Domingo Gonsales to the moon lashed to forty swans.

Yet putting members of the public in space, projected to be difficult, is proving even more difficult than that. Target dates have been pushed back and back. In part that's because there can be no mistakes, and Branson's grand goal of sending a party of A-listers on a 2 ½-hour Mach 3 thrill ride—Tom Hanks, Angelina Jolie and others have signed on—has only added to the pressure. No matter how much dark gratification millions will receive if a spaceship full of celebrities explodes, it would be bad for the company. "NASA has lost about 3% [of its astronauts]," Branson said. ". . . For a government-owned company, you can just about get away with losing 3% of your clients. For a private company you can't really lose anybody."

This got me wondering if on launch days the prayers for success might get a last quarter turn: if there were superstitions attached to spaceflight, things to do for luck. I found that there are. So for example, if Tom Hanks et al. were to emulate Russian cosmonauts, they would urinate on the right rear tire of the vehicle that carries them to the launch pad or, via NASA, they might play blackjack with the tech crew before boarding the flight and ground control would eat peanuts. But I wander from my purpose. The concern of this book lies not with the immediate future but well beyond it, when paying customers are routinely orbiting the Earth like

loose laundry and it's nearing time for the first lunar colonists to embark.

The initial challenge will be deciding who gets to go. The details of that process we can't foresee, but there are one or two things we do know. We know, for instance, that there will be more qualified candidates than experts once believed. Back in the 1950s some scientists thought only acrobats would ever go into space. Or contortionists. Or with luck "very small people." Then someone suggested females: "Women could probably weather long periods of loneliness better," a psychologist explained, "because they are more content to while away the hours dwelling on trivia." Or as Professor Harold Pepinsky of Ohio State University comprehensively put it, the ideal astronaut might well be "a female midget with a PhD in physics."

By contrast, screeners of tomorrow will face a huge applicant pool. They may even be under siege from candidates animated by the principle that it's better to break up with Earth before Earth breaks up with you. In such a press of volunteers, Job One will be weeding out the screwballs. For as former astronaut James Reilly has pointed out, once we start sending non-professionals into space, "We stand a greater chance of someone getting a little nuts."

To learn how this winnowing might be done, I contacted Dr. Patricia Santy, former head of psychiatric selection criteria at NASA, and asked her.

"I wish there were really good psychological tests," Dr. Santy said, "but there aren't."

Given that over the years candidate astronauts have been put through everything from the Millon Clinical Multiaxial Inventory to the Minicog Rapid Assessment Battery, that they've had to Draw-a-Person, give twenty different answers to the question, Who Am I?, and on and on, her reply took me aback. But Dr. Santy explained that, useful as they are, none of these tests can predict for sure how someone will react to actually being in space. She added that during her time at NASA she had learned even less than she might have because astronauts went into full macho lockdown whenever she appeared: "I felt barely tolerated there."

All right, I thought. Then let's go at the problem a different way. When it comes to experiencing spaceflight, what can we learn from the pros in action? What sorts of coping strategies do we see?

One I discovered in a 2007 NASA internal report:

> *Interviews with both flight surgeons and astronauts identified some episodes of heavy use of alcohol by astronauts in the immediate preflight period, which has led to flight safety concerns . . . The medical certification of astronauts for flight duty is not structured to detect such episodes, nor is any medical surveillance*

program by itself likely to detect them or change the
pattern of alcohol use.

That brought back memories. Back in my college days I would sometimes think to myself ahead of a new adventure, "This will be even better if I'm tripping." With LSD I was always wrong. I'd lose track of everything looking at wallpaper that wasn't there. Mescaline, on the other hand, produced the sensation of dreaming what really *was* there, which on the whole I preferred. Sitting on a lake bank watching dragonflies stitch the water on a summer day was astonishing in itself; they didn't have to rearrange themselves into other things. Even threads of anxiety or sadness reinforced the idea that drugs enriched and enlarged the complexity of experience.

I don't think you can make the same argument for being bombed in space. Clearly the goal there is not to feel more but to feel less. This suggests that no matter how tremendous the experience of space travel is—in fact, because it is so tremendous—the gestalt of the thing, the id of the ride, is fear. That's not a disparagement: as we're taught by the age of ten, there is no courage without it.

At any rate, this is something the 50s got right. At the US Army's research center in Dayton, Ohio the architects of manned spaceflight descried at once that terror was the beast in the machine, and they set about trying to analyze its fiber. The first tests were modest enough. For reasons now obscure,

one involved analyzing the "mechanics of fainting" in the opossum. According to the literature the best way to frighten a possum is to shake it, whereupon the animal feigns death, "drools and may discharge a noxious substance from its anal glands." These tests were soon abandoned, but others took their place, escalating in scope and ambition till they vaulted into a sort of scientific Grand Guignol.

The image of a solo astronaut drove a huge amount of isolation and sensory-deprivation research. As it happened, the CIA for reasons of its own was already on top of this: inspired by forms of torture inflicted on US soldiers during the Korean War, the agency was nosing for truffles in the field of annihilating the human mind. In cooperation with Harvard and Boston University it sponsored studies in which, for example, volunteers were placed in "light-proof, soundproof rooms, cardboard tubes surrounding the arms and hands" to see what would happen. What happened were "primitive aggressive fantasies" and "strikingly vivid hallucinations in multiple spheres" along with imaginary things on fire and holes opening in the floor. Impressed by these results, NASA too ran batteries of tests. Soon the line between torturing spies and training astronauts effectively disappeared. It took a couple of years before an air official raised a slow hand to ask, *What does this have to do with being an astronaut?* After all, in outer space "sensory deprivation would be far from complete; the pilot would have jobs to do." Besides, the reports

of bottomless horror were getting monotonous. "Certainly a space man is going to get the quakes," an Air Force physiologist pointed out, "but no worse than those poor wretches who were tossed to the lions in ancient Rome. A fellow can get just so scared and no more."

Much of this grisly saga, like the CIA's corrupt alliance with higher education, isn't really surprising. What I keep wondering about, what I keep trying to get inside of, is the hearts and minds of those test subjects. What on earth put them there? Boredom, patriotism, a death wish? Money? I've tried to imagine my way into one of those isolation chambers—just for a moment—but it's not possible. My experience with drugs doesn't help because the worst trip I ever had was driving a sports car through the kingdom of Babar a lot longer than I wanted to.

But there is one thing that takes me at least a short way into that horror, and it's not even something that happened to me. I once came across a news item about a woman in New Jersey who went to a clinic for an MRI. She lay down, slid smoothly into one of those tunnels and stayed there overnight. The staff turned off the lights and went home accidentally leaving her in the machine.

I've thought of this poor woman more times than I can say. On my one occasion in an MRI tunnel I started screaming in under three minutes. But maybe that's not your worst nightmare. Let's say you had a choice. You could either be the

lady in the tunnel or Air Force captain Joe Kittinger, sent to learn if a person could survive a rocket crackup on the edge of space. In 1960 he pitched backwards from a balloon 20 miles above the earth, free-fell for more than 4 ½ minutes, accelerating to 614 mph, and when his chute finally opened said, "Thank you God, thank you God, thank you God," over and over for a minute and forty-five seconds.

Kittinger's fall was the last of the great wild-ass fear experiments, and since then terror in space isn't something we've considered much. But it's a subject sure to surface when moon colonists are suiting up, for even in the very latest spaceship the ride will be filled with hazards like:

Equipment failure: To date at least fifty-five space missions have been doomed by software errors alone. Mariner 1, launched to explore Venus, came to grief because of a typo.

The Van Allen belts: These are clouds of radiation that hang like Spanish moss between Earth and the moon, capable of swelling without notice "in response to incoming energy from the sun, engulfing satellites and spacecraft."

Space debris: The revolving wheel of space junk which has turned our planet into a sort of down-market Saturn contains 22,000 primary chunks, each under individual surveillance around the clock. They sail along in a haze of tens of millions of smaller bits, any one of which could theoretically pop a hole in a rocket.

Given the level of danger, it's a little surprising that no one who's gone into space so far has totally lost it. There have been shouting matches, a brief mutiny, funks, but no lunging for the bungee cords and tranquillizers, which is NASA protocol for handling psychotics in the sky. On the other hand, virtually all of these 400-plus individuals have been professionals, brilliantly trained. Tomorrow's moon colonists may be less so. Which returns us to the problem of how to pick the right people for the trip.

"Sociopaths might do very well," Dr. Santy offered. "They have excellent survival skills."

Bring them and welcome, but we can't expect them to colonize the moon by themselves. Ways must be found to help regular people relax during the flight.

Ironically, given NASA's resistance to the inner life, Robo-Freud could be one of these. Pioneered by Dr. James Cartreine of the Harvard Medical School, its laconic software is designed to reduce fears and boost optimism in-flight. But the talking cure is being developed primarily for longer trips, say to Mars. How much it would help on a three-day hop isn't clear.

Who cares? What about sex? Yes, it's a ragged possibility. But when futurist Laura Woodmansee calls zero-g sex the "killer app" of space travel, when California's Space Island Group promises "fabulous sex" for the price of a car, when promoters in general swear that before you know it, strenuous tongues will be bursting joy's grape all over the night sky,

they're getting ahead of themselves. As things stand today, the struggle to consummate would be more involving than the sex itself. Inventions to date like the Snuggle Tunnel—described as "a giant slinky covered in velveteen"—don't seem to be good enough yet, nor will everyone want to be steered, nudged and held in place by a third party (the 3-Dolphin Technique). As you might imagine a lot of torrid ingenuity is pouring into this field so by the time colonists get set to fly the problems should mostly be sorted out. We can also expect add-ons like the "zero-g Jacuzzi." According to the designer, John Spencer of California, it is based on the principle that absent gravity, water floats in perfect orbs: "You could have an 8-foot sphere of colored water . . . and people could dive in and float around." Add booze (back to that!) and some "zero-gravity bar glasses" and you've got yourself a party.

As always, shyer souls will hover at the margins. But there another distraction may lurk. Ancient mariners had a name for it: the Call of the Abyss. In the days of the great sailing ships, seamen mesmerized by the swell of the deep would sometimes pitch themselves overboard and be lost. Apparently the same thing can happen in space. In 1965 ground control had to demand that Ed White, America's first spacewalker, return to his capsule, and when he finally did, he called it "the saddest moment of my life." In the 1970s a Russian cosmonaut, hypnotized by what he saw through the window, crept into an airlock undetected and was about to

launch himself into the void when others snatched him back. With a bit of luck—good or bad, who's to say—one of our moon-bound crew might hear the call himself. Bewitched, with untellable adventures in view, he too might slip the air-lock and squeeze outside. Too late, fellow passengers mash themselves against the glass, hands splayed, mouths wide. But even if he could hear them, he wouldn't care, as he glides away with a big fat smile on his face, Ulysses among the stars.

CHAPTER 3 NOTES

33   **nearly came out of her dress:** "Branson Manhandles Kate Moss," *Metro* (June 22, 2009), http://metro .co.uk. Branson has also swung Pamela Anderson and held Ivanka Trump upside down.

      model for Iron Man (Musk): Alan Ohnsman, "A New Henry Ford," [London] *Independent* (July 17, 2013).

      groaned to consume: Brad Stone, "Amazon, the Company That Ate the World," *Bloomberg Businessweek* (September 28, 2011). Also, Brid-Aine Parnell, "Amazon Kingpin's Pocket Rocket Splatters Across Texas," *The Register* (June 9, 2011).

      Where else to reach but up?: Cf. *Chinatown*: Gittes: *Why are you doing it? . . . What could you buy that you can't already afford?* Cross: *The future, Mr. Gittes! The future.* Clip: https://www.youtube.com/watch?v=ppGd-2nEOVQ

      smaller companies frisking at the margins: One of these, First Advantage, has announced plans to marry couples in parabolas at one-ten-thousandth their normal weight.

34   **lashed to forty swans:** Francis Godwin, op. cit.

      you can't really lose anybody: Chris Matyszczyk, "Branson on Galactic: We Can't Afford to Kill Tom Hanks or Angelina Jolie," *CNET* (February 23, 2014).

      urinate on the right rear tire: Nancy Atkinson, "Expedition 34's Ride to Space Rolls to Launchpad," (December 23, 2015), https://www.universetoday.com.

      play blackjack with the tech crew: Alan Murphy, "The losing hand: tradition and superstition in spaceflight," *The Space Review* (May 27, 2008). Branson in particular might be attracted to such rituals if for no other reason

than to counteract his decision to locate Spaceport America in New Mexico's desert of Jornada del Muerto ("single day's journey of the dead man").

35 **acrobats . . . contortionists:** Amy Shira Teitel, "Designing the Perfect Astronaut," (December 7, 2010), www.vintagespace.wordpress.com.

dwelling on trivia: Daniel Lang, "Man in Space," *The New Yorker* (November 15, 1958). Curiously, another reason offered in support of using female astronauts was that "women have notoriously strong ties to reality."

female midget with a PhD in physics: Ibid.

someone getting a little nuts: "NASA Trains Astronauts to Bind, Tranquilize Unstable Crewmates," *Fox News* (February 25, 2007). The chances of a crack-up may have increased because so many of us have lost the comfort of religion. Broadly speaking, a 15th-century serf would have climbed into a rocket with more confidence than you or I.

36 **but there aren't:** Dr. Patricia Santy, author interview.

to the question, Who Am I?: Among the multitude of other tests NASA has administered over the years was the Minnesota Multiphasic Personality Inventory, which required yes or no responses to statements like, "I often worry about my health," and "Strangers keep trying to hurt me."

I felt barely tolerated there: Dr. Santy, author interview.

37 **change the pattern of alcohol use:** Maria Newman and John Schwartz, "Report Uncovers Astronauts' Heavy Alcohol Use," *New York Times* (July 27, 2007).

the complexity of experience: With hallucinogens I could also protest the Vietnam war without leaving my room.

38 **"mechanics of fainting" in the opossum:** Lloyd Mallan, *Men, Rockets and Space Rats* (Mesner, 1958).

substance from its anal glands: Joe Eaton, "Endangered Opossums Really Do Play Dead," *Berkeley Daily Planet* (February 1, 2005).

isolation and sensory-deprivation research: H. Ben-aroya, ed. *Lunar Settlements* (CRC Press, 2010).

strikingly vivid hallucinations in multiple spheres: Stuart Grassian, "Psychiatric Effects of Solitary Confinement," Washington University *Journal of Law and Policy* 22 (2006).

sensory deprivation would be far from complete: A British Air Ministry official speaking at an international symposium on outer space in 1958. He thought being an astronaut would more likely resemble "certain patterns of political imprisonment."

40 **last of the great wild-ass fear experiments:** The most important experiment-in-waiting could not then be run. When President Kennedy took office, there was still a general fear in the business that weightlessness might obliterate reason altogether or kill you if you sneezed. The first effort to understand its effects was made by Hubertus Strughold in 1928. At that time Strughold had not yet become chief of Aeromedical Research for the German Luftwaffe, nor had he overseen the torture and murder of prisoners at Dachau, done seminal research for the US Air Force, godfathered the pressure suit for American astronauts and earned the honorific "Father of Aviation Medicine." His weightlessness test consisted of anesthetizing his buttocks and executing acrobatic maneuvers in a small plane. The idea was to deprive himself of that "seat-of-the-pants" feeling and see what he learned. It wasn't much.

came to grief because of a typo: Comins, *Hazards of Space Travel* (Villard, 2007).

engulfing satellites and spacecraft: "NASA's Van Allen Probes Reveal Previously Undetected Radiation Belt Around the Earth," (February 28, 2013), https://universal wavetheory.wordpress.com. Trippy animation at: "NASA | Van Allen Probes Reveal Previously Undetected Radiation

Belt Around Earth": www.youtube.com/watch?v=XKC
MaJBXmzY

pop a hole in a rocket: See, e.g., Ran Levi, "The Orbital
Menace—Space Garbage," http://www.thefutureofthings
.com. In orbit even the smallest bits are travelling thousands of miles an hour.

41 **handling psychotics in the sky:** "NASA Trains Astronauts to Bind, Tranquilize Unstable Crewmates," *Fox
News* (February 25, 2007).

Sociopaths might do very well: Dr. Santy, author interview.

Robo-Freud: Austin Modine, "Scientists prep robo-Freud
for depressed astronauts," *The Register* (October 28, 2008).

"killer app" of space travel: Laura Woodmansee, "Sex in
Space: Imagine the Possibilities," *National Space Society*
(February 8, 2006).

for the price of a car: "Sex in space offered in first space
island honeymoon suite," *Marie Claire* (December 11,
2007).

42 **giant slinky covered in velveteen:** As featured on the ar-
resting blog *Arse Elektronica*, which explores topics at the
intersection of sex and technology, e.g., "What goes into
the extraction of raw resources, such as the rubber tree
plantations of South America, that make our condoms
and catsuits?" and "Can fucking charge a battery?" Un-
convincing demonstration of Snuggle Tunnel with dolls:
https://www.youtube.com/watch?v=Jl4VODxGUoA

3-Dolphin Technique: To investigate further visit "Sex in
Space Resources" at: https://archive.li/yhVcW

zero-g Jacuzzi: Michael Behar, "The Zero-G Spot," *Outside* (December 5, 2006).

zero-gravity bar glasses: Courtesy of one Sam Coniglio.

the saddest moment of my life: Ben Evans, "Examina-
tions of Some Kind: The Walk of Ed White," (June 6, 2012),

http://www.americaspace.com/2012/06/06/examinations
-of-some-kind-the-walk-of-ed-white/.

43 **launch himself into the void:** James Oberg, "Extra-Ve-
hicular Adventures, Risky Space Walking," (2010), http://
www.jamesoberg.com/09012005riskywalking_shr.html.

CHAPTER 4

SHELTER

I don't know the particular moment when librarians threw in the towel. I don't know if they held a convention and decided, "Fuck it, we're not whispering anymore," or the yakking of the patrons overwhelmed them or what. But I haven't taken it well. I miss the old days. It's as if noise-wise we've trampled down the last fence.

It's not the world's worst problem, I realize. Fish would laugh if they could hear me complain although they can't because thanks to sonar and the auriferous hungers of mankind parts of the ocean sound like New York City on a summer day. On land it's almost impossible now to record a full day's unbroken natural sound anywhere in the world. It's as if the 7 billion of us on the planet had formed the worst high-school band you could possibly imagine. But that's just what we are, devoted amateurs—which is to say that the noise we've been making isn't as loud as it could be.

49

Enter the LRAD 500X Sound Cannon. The LRAD, aka Long Range Acoustic Hailing Device, delivers precision levels of hearing loss with a signature blast—a baby crying played backwards combined with two competing sirens—that can put whole crowds flat on the ground unable to crawl away. Alternatively, a Henske Systems unit emits pulses of sound that nail all twenty-two bones of the skull "optionally preceded by legal warnings where applicable."

And so I turn with deep and honest envy to our lunar colonists as I picture them at the moment of arrival. Each in turn descends the ship's ladder and drops to the ground in a puff. Two or three begin to move about. One scuffing through the dust goes into spasms from the static electricity. But most simply stand transfixed by the almost Trappist silence of the moon.

Saying I envy that quiet doesn't mean I could handle it. Years ago I attended a three-day yoga retreat in upstate New York. I'd never done yoga before, but it didn't look hard, or at least not competitive, so I figured, Why not? I'd been torching my system with mescaline and scotch and thought it could use a rest. But I did almost no research on the place so I was stunned to learn on arrival that we were forbidden to speak. You could write something on a piece of paper if vitally necessary, but otherwise communication was confined to smiles. My reaction to this discovery was shock followed by panic. I'm not that social ordinarily, but the thought of being mute for

seventy-two hours was like suddenly being encased in a tube. A few hours in I was wondering if I might start shouting or gibbering, uncorking a hitherto dormant pocket of mental illness. By the next morning I was sunk in resentment toward the Zen fascists running the retreat. Then I got sick. As I said, knowing nothing of what to expect, I also wasn't prepared for how limited the menu would be, most of it variations on one thing, bulgur I think, and the diet change combined with the sudden cut-off of booze, drugs and cigarettes put me flat on my cot with a swimming fever. Sick and mute. One thing, however, was clear in my mind. My body craved something and I knew what it was so I hauled myself outdoors and stumbled down the long slope to the kitchen. Several people were there preparing the next round of bulgur. I handed one of them the scrap of paper I'd brought with me. On it were the words, "Can I please have an orange?" The cook—younger than me, almost a kid—took my pencil, turned the page over, wrote and passed it back. "No," it read. The next thing I remember I was blundering down a road away from the retreat consumed with the thought that if I just walked far enough sooner or later I'd come across a place that sold fruit. By that point I wasn't sure which I wanted more, the orange itself or to say out loud, "I'd like an orange," but I never got to find out because eventually a car slid up beside me and in perfect silence I was returned Patrick McGoohan–like to the compound.

That's as close as I've ever come to living in space, and it's one more proof that I wouldn't do well there. But for those who thrive on negative virtues the moon will be fantastic. Just like the effects of Midgley's inventions, the brutality of noise will disappear. On the moon you can't hear a party horn. This makes me wonder, sentimentally I know, whether some who settle there might achieve a sort of Zen from without. Maybe, in the words of a Persian mystic, those lucky few will be able to "stop weaving and see how the pattern improves."

Now and then, I mean, once the work gets going.

So what tasks will our lunar settlers face first? Well, forward motion to start with, something we haven't seen much of in the past. Indeed, to think that man has walked on the moon is a woolly-minded view of the facts. The movements executed so far as tracked by the Huntsville, Alabama Space and Rocket Center are:

The Bunny Hop
The Side-to-Side
The Slow Motion Jog

I don't mean by this to disparage those iconic space suits from the 60s. They served wonderfully for the time and offered more style and mobility than earlier designs had led us to expect:

Lunar suit for space explorer

A spaceman could use this suit while exploring the moon—and even rest in it if he's on a long hike. It is equipped with retractable tripod legs that will hold it up off the ground and a built-in seat that he can curl up on while easing his tired feet.

The suit is made of aluminum, has a circular plastic window and nylon-coated neoprene arms and legs. The tank strapped to the back supplies oxygen and contains a carbon-dioxide absorbent. The controls are inside the cylinder along with shelves of food for lengthy trips. Tools the wearer could use would be similar to those lying on the ground. The suit was built by Republic Aviation, weighs 120 pounds, which on the low-gravity Moon would be equivalent to 20 on Earth.

Yet the fact remains that these gas-pressurized models were heavy and clumsy and made shoulder surgery routine. Tomorrow's moon pioneers will wear something quite different, something along the lines of the BioSuit now in development at MIT. A "second skin" of plastics threaded with nickel and titanium, the BioSuit works on the principle of counter-pressure, which means shrink-wrapping flesh that would otherwise expand away from the bone. Add a helmet with

flip-down visor, 3D cameras and digital reads and you're all set. In a BioSuit you could strap on wings and cross the moon like a heron. Or cross-country ski, which is what Harrison Schmitt, the last man on the moon, recommends. I can certainly picture that: in Maine I've often seen folks breezing through the frosty woods like that, though they'd have to adjust their technique in space since the moon is a wilderness of holes. So if I, for example, were to trade in my wings for skis and push off—*thrust, thrust, thrust*—and I overshot the lip of the Aitken Basin near the south pole, while it's true that my rate of acceleration downward would be just 1/6th that on Earth, falling 8 miles would get me going at a pretty good clip, so that eventually the curious gathered at the rim would see a tiny puff of dust below caused by what's called terminal impact velocity. Posted warnings for every hole and hollow would require more than half a million signs, not likely even for sites already named for astronomers, philosophers, Julius Caesar, Michael Jackson or for the right price you:

Nothing Could Be Greater Than To Own Your Own Crater!™

But for colonists the slaloming will have to wait. The first thing they'll need to do is start making themselves a home— terraforming, to use the term of art, the process of turning a celestial body that's uninhabitable into one that can sustain human life. You might think that would be easy since

we're demonstrated experts at reverse terraforming, and on the moon we'll be doing the same thing only backwards. It won't be that simple though. Fortunately there's lots of water. Water! Who knew? "Never predicted"—"profound discovery"—in 2009 three centuries of settled opinion exploded when those two probes hit the south pole. Extracting the stuff won't be easy, but there it is.

Thanks to the robot vanguard, there might even be a few buildings already up. Via technology's new darling, 3D printing, the bots themselves could crank out some "extraterrestrial housing using in situ materials" ahead of time—multi-nozzle the lunacrete, paint it, pipe it, then on to the next unit. When humans join in, construction will be more complex, but they won't do the usual things. You can't just take a jackhammer to romance and heathen mythologies and get good results. You can't drill on the moon at all. In a vacuum the heat would be so intense it would fuse the equipment. You can't blast. The debris would shoot out like a nail bomb with nothing to slow it down. Oils and hydraulic fluids won't function. Which leaves us with what? A member of the Army Corps of Engineers believes we may have to use tools from the 19th century, and when I spoke with Prof. Madhu Thangavelu, a designer of off-world architecture, he looked even further back. "When it comes to building and hauling," he said, "we have much to learn from the ancient Egyptians."

Remembering who did that building and hauling, I suddenly wondered if the moon of tomorrow might be built by slaves. It's an old, old story: an innocent lured by a tinkling bell of promises, then driven like a tent peg into involuntary servitude. Once you're on the moon, what's to prevent it? Come to that, what about the negative impact of isolation itself? Some psychologists fret that faced with a life of silence, exile and cunning, our colonists might slowly come unstuck. Part of this concern derives from studies in Antarctica, where remote settlers living in extreme temperatures have sometimes suffered a hormonal imbalance called T3 syndrome, aka "Going Toast." "I loved watching people fall apart," one participant recalled. "I loved falling apart myself. When I became Toasty . . . I shaved my eyebrows off. I was drinking liquid morphine with someone named Big Hand George."

To me that sounds pretty cool. More risky on the moon though, so I guess we should try to figure out if it could happen there. Viewing the question from the vantage point of ignorance—the world's most crowded piece of property—I think not. What the worriers forget is that from the moment they arrive, settlers will be ferociously scrutinized 24/7 by millions on Earth via computers and VR links. Throw in reality TV and the rest and I have to think that lunar colonists will be the least isolated people in the history of the universe. Performance anxiety should be the concern. Or maybe not, because—think this through with me here—by then they

may be so used to being watched it's simply part of life. We're well on the road now, growing used to surveillance, upping the dose, the way some in the past have ingested increasing amounts of arsenic to build up a tolerance. Rasputin did that, nibbling more and more to protect himself against poisoning (although as it turned out, he would have been better off stabbing himself once in a while). I bought a bottle of vitamins with extra iron at Rite-Aid recently, and the next day I was getting personalized ads for vitamins with extra iron on You-Tube. At first I felt spooked but then weirdly peaceful. I could feel the glass being installed in my head pane by pane. *Mi cerebro es tu cerebro.* Horrifying, sure, but perhaps surrender is the only way to retain a certain spaciousness of mind. Privacy is so clenched.

Sometimes settlers could crawl into their tetrahedral inflatable modules and pretend they're alone. Or hexahedral, octahedral, etc., for when it comes to housing, lunacrete's not the only way to go. However, to block out the radiation each of these pop-up units will have to be covered in regolith 10 feet thick. Which, someone is bound to observe, is a lot of fucking regolith, leading someone else perhaps to point and say, "See that lava tube? Why don't we just put it in there?"

The moon was once a blazing ball of confusion. I say that although like most big facts it's easier to accept as an idea than to picture full-force. I believe it more than I comprehend it, if you know what I mean. It's like visiting the Col-

osseum in Rome. A couple of years ago my kids and I were accompanying a tour guide there who was dressed disheartingly like Marvin the Martian. He would stop now and then and, pointing at spots in the vast bowl below, recite tales of floating armadas and ostrich wars and all sorts of baroque slaughter. I looked hard trying to picture these things, to see them fully in my mind, but I didn't even come close. What registered on my retina was absence, the ruin of what was once a ruin. The imagination soars, but it also shrivels. Sometimes you just can't get there.

The moon at least has frozen lava to prove its case, thousands upon thousands of channels and caves, and it's into one of these that our colonists are now dragging their stuff. Here's where our future on the moon lies, much of it, inside and way, way down . . .

Just imagining my head in a helmet makes me feel like the Man in the Iron Mask, and now we're descending into the very bowels of the moon where claustrophobia is the serpent king. It's a good thing most people don't have this problem. Down the centuries we've chalked up masses of troglodyte experience in dank, square tunnels and chapels of skulls, plenty of preparation for the world into which we are about to step. Yet the sight will be fantastically different from anything we've known.

I'm speaking now of the far future, some indeterminate number of decades after the first lunar settlement—if pres-

ent plans come true. When the elevator drops, settles and the doors part, they will reveal something resembling a supercollider lab lost in the Amazon. "It will be like living in a greenhouse jungle," Dr. Bernard Foing says, for from the first tulip on bud-watch via satellite feed (something he passionately favors), he foresees a powerful psychological need in colonists to surround themselves with plants as a comfort, a dimensional nourishment, amid the glazed rock and gizmos and weaving droids.

Through the fronds we glimpse apartments hewn from the living rock with communal kitchens adjoining. Deep in— and we can go deep, deep in, into caves "like vast cathedrals, if a cathedral can be imagined that is thousands of times longer than it is wide and high"—we find shops, galleries, fountains, everything in short from VR adventures to bowling. Like other forms of recreation the hookers will probably locate here as well. Workers from above slipping down for a lunar nooner may not find them as glamorous as the winged prostitutes of Luxo-Volupto, but you never know.

How much of this vast ambition will be realized none can tell, but of one thing we can be sure. "Scientists here," Dr. Thangavelu says, "we go home, we play the violin, we paint, we sculpt. The same things have to happen there." Which is to say, it won't be long before settlers underground are making art.

Cave painting is almost too obvious to mention. Thirty-two thousand years ago humans by torchlight filled a cav-

ern in Europe with representations of horses, mammoths, rhinoceri, stunning in themselves and a gong in the mind because something is happening here and you don't know what it is. A cave dweller on the moon, evolutionarily far advanced over his distant cousins, will scratch location coordinates and EAT ME on the walls, but also, if life there rekindles even a bit of the old awe, pictures of the Great Bear and other creatures outlined by the stars. At least it's pretty to think so.

The Romans paved Tunisian caves with mosaics, a perfect union of aesthetics and mathematics. Maybe some soulstruck nerd will do the same. All right, I'm designing my own moon now, but you're free to do likewise. Let me just point out that "flamenco"—which translates as "music of the displaced"—was born in the caves of southern Spain, and we know what a cultural cyclone that became. Whether cave dwellers on the moon also create a fiery new dance form we'll have to see. But sooner or later, dance they will.

CHAPTER 4 NOTES

49 **librarians threw in the towel:** This critique does not apply
to the Falmouth Memorial Library, Falmouth, Maine.
sound like New York City on a summer day: William J.
Broad, "A Rising Tide of Noise Is Now Easy to See," *New
York Times* (December 10, 2012).
full day's unbroken natural sound: Kim Tingley, "Whispers of the Wild," *New York Times* (March 15, 2012).

50 **LRAD 500X Sound Cannon:** Shaviv, "Mad Science
Project of the Week 9," (May 8, 2008), https://www
.dailykos.com/stories/2008/5/8/511938/-Mad-Science
-Project-of-the-Week-9-wherein-loud-noise-is-found-to
-be-annoying. Also: Marshall Sella, "The Sound of Things
to Come," *New York Times Magazine* (March 23, 2003).
legal warnings where applicable: "Sonic Crowd Management," (August 25, 2009), https://sonicwarfare.wordpress
.com/2009/08/25/sonic-crowd-management/.

52 **more proof that I wouldn't do well there:** I'm no longer
so sure of that since stumbling upon a Russian website, a
you and your health–type blog, where I found this:

*With respect to the lunar geriatrics, the most of us will spare
neither money nor effort to extension own lives. Perhaps a
small force of gravity (on the Moon, it is six times less than
Earth's) can extend certainly much easier life in the inevitable for everyone age when the need to move their od-ry-
ahlevshee body becomes almost unmanageable . . .*

All right, it was one of those auto-translation things, but
you get the idea. A revolutionary form of decrepitude. Ev-

erything light and easy. Dignity preserved. Too late for me of course: long before the rockets are ready I'll be blithering among the hollyhocks. Still, it's nice to imagine. I think of the rest-home shuffle awaiting me here; then I look at the moon and there I am, all suited up and skipping, perhaps a bit higher than I'd like but still, the feeling, and when I fall—oops—instead of shattering my hip, I settle as gently as an autumn leaf.

stop weaving and see how the pattern improves: Rumi, 13th-century Sufi mystic.

The Slow Motion Jog: "Train Like an Astronaut at Space School," www.ivicon.com.au.

53   **Illustration, "lunar suit for space explorer":** *Popular Science* (January 1961).

shoulder surgery routine: "This New Form-Fitting Space Suit Could Revolutionize How Astronauts Move In Space," *Business Insider* (December 13, 2013).

Re: shrink-wrapping flesh in low gravity: Jim Algar, "MIT's pressurized 'BioSuit' ensures astronauts are comfortable in their second skin," *Tech Times* (September 19, 2014).

54   **what Harrison Schmitt . . . recommends:** James Randerson, "Good skiing on the moon, says Apollo veteran," *The Guardian* (February 18, 2007).

Aitken Basin: One of the deepest craters in the solar system. Vivid acid-flash topography pix at http://www .astronomy.com/news/2015/10/mound-near-lunar-south -pole-formed-by-unique-volcanic-process

half a million signs: https://museum.wales/2482/

Julius Caesar, Michael Jackson: Ben Leach, "Moon Crater Named After Michael Jackson," *The Telegraph* (September 7, 2009). Jackson already had substantial lunar holdings in the Sea of Vapors and the Lake of Dreams.

Than To Own Your Own Crater!™: Buy here: http://www .lunarregistry.com

55   **profound discovery:** See, e.g., David L. Chandler, "Ben
      Weiss discusses what a wet moon might mean," *MIT News
      Office* (September 30, 2009).

      a few buildings already up: During the space race it
      was still unclear if the lunar surface was a surface. Some
      thought the dust might be miles deep. In 1959 John S.
      Rinehart of the Colorado School of Mines designed a
      floating moonbase for astronauts just in case. Two years
      later Arthur C. Clarke published a novel, *A Fall of Moon-
      dust*, in which a shipload of tourists sinks into the regolith
      Das Boot–style.

      technology's new darling, 3D printing: Applied to hous-
      ing, a particular variant called "contour crafting" was
      conceived by Dr. Behrokh Khoshnevis of USC. For his
      TED talk on the subject see "Contour Crafting: Automat-
      ed Construction": https://www.youtube.com/watch?v=Jd
      bJP8Gxqog

      multi-nozzle the lunacrete: By some accounts lunacrete,
      a regolith-based variation, will have ten times the com-
      pressive and tensile strength of concrete: Ian O'Neill,
      "Building a Moon Base, Part 3 – Structural Design," (De-
      cember 26, 2015), https://www.universetoday.com/12864
      /building-a-base-on-the-moon-part-3-structural-design/.

      fuse the equipment: Ian O'Neill, "Building a Moon Base,
      Part 1 – Challenges and Hazards," (April 26, 2016), https://
      www.universetoday.com/12726/building-a-base-on-the
      -moon-challenges-and-hazards/.

      tools from the 19th century: Guy Gugliotta, "US Shoots
      for Moon to Make It to Mars," *Washington Post* (March 27,
      2006).

      much to learn from the ancient Egyptians: Prof. Madhu
      Thangavelu, Dept. of Astronautical Engineering, USC, au-
      thor interview.

56   **driven like a tent peg into involuntary servitude:** Some
      have suggested that, although not technically slaves, lunar

colonists might find themselves under the thumb of impersonal corporations. This can't happen though because there aren't any. As we've come to learn (*Citizens United v. Federal Election Commission*, 2010), corporations are people too. In fact they're the luckiest people in the world because they don't eat, sleep, fornicate, urinate, defecate or hold up trembling hands against the imprint of death. So they can concentrate on making a really good living.

Big Hand George: *Harper's* (November 2007).

via computers and VR links: David Schrunk et al., *The Moon: Resources, Future Development and Settlement* (Praxis, 2007).

57   **increasing amounts of arsenic:** John Parascandola, "The Arsenic Eaters of Styria," http://ultimatehistoryproject .com/arsenic-eaters.html.

Rasputin did that: V.P. Singh, *Metal Toxicity and Tolerance in Plants and Animals* (Sarup & Son, 2008).

tetrahedral inflatable modules: Ian O'Neill, "Building a Moon Base: Part 2 – Habitat Concepts," (February 9, 2008), https://www.universetoday.com/12758/building-a -base-on-the-moon-part-2-habitat-concepts/.

regolith 10 feet thick: Guy Gugliotta, "Can We Survive on the Moon?," *Discover Magazine* (March 2007).

59   **It will be like living in a greenhouse jungle:** Dr. Bernard Foing, European Space Agency, author interview.

like vast cathedrals: Adrian Berry, *The Next 500 Years: Life in the Coming Millennium* (W. H. Freeman, 1996). More recently: Arlin Crofts, *The New Moon* (Cambridge University Press, 2014) writes that some caves are so large that "one can engineer spaces sufficient to engender feelings of being outside." But till we get down there it's all a bit vague.

VR adventures to bowling: John Carlin, "Fly Me to the Moon," *The Independent* (March 18, 1998). Given some

debate regarding the long-term stability of the rock, underground bowling could be one of the worst ideas ever.

winged prostitutes of Luxo-Volupto: Anonymous, *The Travels of Hildebrand Bowman, Esquire* (London: 1778).

we paint, we sculpt: Prof. Madhu Thangavelu, author interview.

humans by torchlight filled a cavern: The Chauvet-Pont-d'Arc Cave in southern France, discovered in 1994. See *Cave of Forgotten Dreams*, Werner Herzog, dir. A cheesy title for a wonderful documentary.

60 **paved Tunisian caves with mosaics:** G.S. Golany, *Earth-Sheltered Dwellings in Tunisia* (Univ. of Delaware Press, 1988).

born in the caves of southern Spain: Maki Navaja, "Flamenco 33 – The Origins," (December 28, 2011), http://casamaki.com. Smoldering performance of the dance itself: Celina Zambon, "Flamenco Dance": http://www.youtube.com/watch?v=xqxJMCQxb_Q

CHAPTER 5

FOOD

Any student of the moon is inevitably struck by how long it has been entwined with the dream of giant vegetables. Why it has I'm not sure, whether its dominion over Earth farming somehow applied, but with the arrival of the telescope the notion of jumbo lunar plants took off. In the late 18th century William Herschel—a brilliant astronomer, lens maker, discoverer of the planet Uranus—spied what he took to be rampant vegetation "of a much larger size on the Moon than it is here." In 1835 an electrifying series of articles in the *New York Sun* reported the presence of lunar vegetables, "every imaginable production of a bounteous soil," so big as to be detectable through telescopes at a distance of a quarter million miles, and squatted in the midst of which creatures with translucent wings could be seen ravening "a large yellow fruit like a gourd"—this a hoax, as it turned out, but so attuned to the popular mind it transcended fact, reinforced

soon after by Jules Verne, inspirer of the Offenbach operetta *Le voyage dans la lune,* whose signature stage trick involved plants shooting suddenly way, way up, higher and higher, until they produced—*poof, poof, poof*—flowers and fruit. Come the 1920s, and one Dr. Pickering of Harvard (no relation to the lunar bomb enthusiast) announced that shadows on the moon were caused by the raging vitality of its plants. His conclusions were puffed in the press alongside speculative art such as, "Mushroom Growths 1,000 Feet High on the Surface of the Moon With Earth Men Crawling Among Them, Looking Like Ants in a Field of Wheat."

All very odd, but whatever made the moon the go-to zone for giant crops, you'd think that by, say, the Eisenhower administration, the scientific community would have taken the idea and poured it down the lav. Not so. Nourished by meadow muffins of paranoia, big moon food shot to new heights of eidetic splendor in the early years of the Cold War.

People go on about the Belle Époque or Paris in the 20s, but my favorite decade has got to be the 50s in the United States. Not to live through. I did that and it wasn't so good. Growing up in the shadow of the bomb was like a grossly premature course in philosophy: *Why am I alive? Why now?* Sometimes I wondered if I'd been chosen by God to serve as a witness to the obliteration of mankind. On the other hand I didn't think nine-year-old Episcopalians would be picked for that. As a preacher's kid, this confusion—whether to be

reassured by religion or terrorized by it—could plunge me into weird glooms, the best solace from which I found in a series of hats: my cowboy hat, my Davey Crockett coonskin cap, my Mickey Mouse Club beanie with the big ears. That's when I learned that the right hat can improve one's outlook materially.

At any rate, that was the 1950s as lived. Viewed from the promontory of time all these years later, they appear something else altogether. Even our fear looks beguiling. At this remove I can see the geology of it, its glints and patterns, the iridescent veins running through the rock. Reviving monster moon food was one of them. This time, however, it came with a difference. This time we weren't going to find it on the moon (*what were they thinking?*). We were going to grow it there ourselves. Unless the enemy did it first. And they were about to! They had the specs! After the triumph of Sputnik, you'll recall, the Soviets announced plans to construct a lunar city. It would be glass-domed, they said, with aluminum sliding doors. Now Prof. Varvarov of the Soviet Astronautics Section went even further: he revealed that the 30-pound Communists living in it would be "self-sufficient as far as food is concerned" because, thanks to the light touch of lunar gravity, Earth vegetables would grow fantastically big there. Radishes would tower like palm trees. Onions would produce sprouts 33 feet long.

Credit: John Cote

This claim cast doubt on the entire Soviet enterprise—or would have if some Western experts hadn't believed the same thing. In a *New York Times* interview British hydroponics expert J. W. W. H. Sholto Douglas concurred that on lunar farms "sap will almost stream up into foliage and fruit. So we would have gigantic cabbages, carrots and apples." Exciting news ordinarily, but these astonishments were about to fall into the wrong hands. Americans were used to viewing the Soviets as sallow and malnourished, another consequence of their loser way of life. Nobody wanted to face Russians full of vitamins.

What to do? How to respond? Sad to report, the best the US could think of was to speed up research on algae. I don't know if you've ever looked at algae on a plate, but if you have, I'll bet you didn't care that some strains of it are wildly nutritious, that they're stuffed with protein along with mega-doses of B vitamins, Vitamin E, iron, potassium and so on. You didn't care that it grows like a dream. You said it's spinach and you said the hell with it. Nevertheless, a beleaguered NASA fell upon it as the future Vitameatavegamin of outer space, easy to grow, easy to eat: "Nutrients for algae would be supplied by human wastes. The algae, in turn, will become food for the crew." But that's just where the problem lay. Even if that cycle had been more genteelly described, anything that breeds easily in urine can never hope for popularity. When word of the plan got around Cape Canaveral, there was pushback from the astronaut pool. Someone back in the test kitchen then proposed a compromise: perhaps intermediate forms of life—snails, eels, rabbits, goats—could go into space with the astronauts. The animals would eat the algae, and the crew would eat them. Alas for initiative: "Such suggestions overlook the enormous task of recycling feathers, hair, hide, horns and offal through the closed system . . ."

Here again we encounter the great themes of the period: a whirlwind of new ideas, the *mysterium tremendum* of spaceflight, and both sides, East and West, just barking. In fairness I have to say that some of their instincts turned out to be right.

Today "going hydro" is still very much in prospect for growing vegetables on the moon. In this regard pot growers, aggressive innovators here, may have a lot to teach: "We use soilless mediums to create the perfect sponge for holding oxygen, water and nutrients to produce serious yields of frosty buds..."

My grandfather in Georgia used to grow vegetables. Out back of the house, on land banked by the humid scent of pines, a hired man with an old white mule plowed each spring, but otherwise my grandfather did everything himself. Well into his nineties he put out 200 tomato plants each spring. He dug every hole, drove every stake, tied every vine. He would pretend I was helping by getting my knees dirty, and then we'd rustle out among the corn, yellow squash, and zucchini to check how many the critters had chewed. There were watermelons too and over near the driveway a dozen huge fig trees, temperamental that far north, which I thought were very unfair to him. By July the kitchen filled with this bounty, crowding the sills, the counters, the top of the refrigerator, creating a dark aroma of soil and linoleum that to me was the smell of summer...

Sorry, I drifted. I was speaking of, or about to speak of, purple food in tanks.

At the Kennedy Space Center in Houston, romaine lettuce, Swiss chard, Chinese cabbage and the like are ripening in cross-rays of red and blue light, this to maximize chlorophyll production as some lunar gardens will likely do. No surprise

then that "the vegetables look weird," as space horticulturist Gioia Massa put it to me, which is to say not so much alive as undead. What struck me more though was how many are engineered to be small. Small! Dwarf wheat, dwarf citrus, dwarf peppers and plum trees—the last of which Massa described as "pretty dwarf and very productive"—a world of small is headed for slo-mo nurture on tomorrow's astro-farm. This flips the old moon-food paradigm on its head, not to mention the one here on Earth, where bigger and faster is what we're all about. According to the trade journal *Poultry Science*, if people grew at the same rate as a mass-market chicken, a 6 ½-pound newborn baby would weigh 660 pounds in two months. I know that's not a vegetable, but Jesus Christ.

Yet when it comes to lunar agriculture, I'm not sure we should bet the farm on dwarf. We should also, I think, be stockpiling masses of seeds on the moon just in case. It's good to hear that Norway's Svalbard Global Seed Vault has stored a million varieties deep in the permafrost to replace whatever we annihilate. But a close enough strike would annihilate the vault, and that could leave moon farmers on a very thin thread. At Jamestown, the first American colony, survivors of the winter of 1609 were reduced to eating their dead. That's less likely to happen off-world. If nothing else, cannibalism on the moon would be a logistical nightmare. Still . . .

This is not to say that all lunar flesh is off the table. Anything is possible given enough technology and enthusiasm for

meat, a feeling best expressed perhaps by the West African word *gouamba*, meaning "meat hunger," or more precisely, "I am sick of food. I want meat. I care for nothing else." Sadly it's not so easy to feel that these days. Given all the health talk, very few of us can eat red meat now without getting mentally involved in it, even if it's only defensively ("I'm eating this and fuck you"). But then all food is haunted now, one way or another. I'm at the market, standing in front of whatever, the kale, thinking how much do I need and what will I make with it, ruminating in a light fog of that kale scare wherever it was when those people died. When it comes to toxins, I'm not sure there's much difference now between feeling and fearing them. Either way there are approximately 37.2 trillion terrorist cells in the human body.

In one way at least eating meat on the moon will be less fraught than here: the animal-rights issues go away. Dollops of livestock would ship from Earth to be coaxed into steaks and chops in lunar labs—a variant I suppose on what self-righteous hunters call "meat that hasn't been lied to." The stuff is coming, no question. Someone chewed and swallowed the first *in vitro* beefburger, built by a Dutch team, at a press conference in 2013.

Similarly, lunar colonists may enjoy an ectype of milk, aka "cow in a column," as opposed to the regular kind my daughter calls "liquid flesh."

But this doctoring and fiddling brings us to the question on which all else depends. Whatever forms moon food takes, there will be no such thing as natural. All off-world agriculture—and thus the entire human experiment in space—will rise or fall on genetic modification.

A sobering thought, no? In the implacable rise of GMO foods it's business, not science, that has predictably seized control of the wheel, and while they may tell us that, for example, a GMO pear related to a natural pear the way a movie is "inspired by true events" is safe, nobody's sure. And if it's not safe:

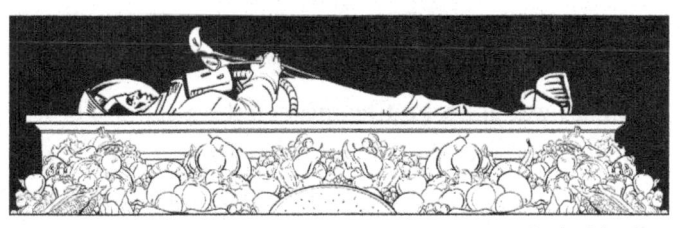

Credit: John Cote

In short, we have to hope that a profit-driven behemoth will be in exact sync with the public good, something we haven't seen much of so far. But if the thing does work, the moon will showcase it best. Growing food there means no ecology to trash, no floods and droughts, no more unsanctioned seeds skipping into the wild. Nor will GMOs add to the "reliable declines" in the food value of forty-three fruits and vegeta-

bles in the United States due to chemicals and soil depletion, nor will it lengthen the list of 250+ non-organic additives approved for use by the National Organics Standards Board because "organic" even as a jargon word will have ceased to apply. Also, GMO foods of the future will look fabulous. Designer Mariah Wright has created gorgeous Audubon-type pictures of plants which, "speculative biologists" tell us, are racing toward us like stars toward a rocket ship. On the moon breadfruit with enhanced bleeding capabilities, self-packaging strawberries and carnivorous wheat, dwarfed, could turn greenhouses into galleries.

Yes, yes, you say, that's all very well. But what about Coke and pizza?

Here's a clue to their level of interest: In much the same way that Sir Isaac Newton and Gottfried Leibniz, working independently, conceived calculus, Coca-Cola and Pizza Hut have both sunk R&D money into learning if it's technologically possible to beam their logos onto a full moon. (The answer: not so far.) To the complainers out there, pugnacious "attorney/explorer" J. H. Heubert says: "What's so wrong with [it]? If the moon naturally, coincidentally had a Pizza Hut logo on it instead of a 'man in the moon' face, environmentalists would clamor to preserve it."

At last report Domino's and Pizza Hut were in a war of words over which franchise would take the moon first, Domino's Pizza Japan projecting the cost at $21.7 billion:

All in all then we've got a two-tiered meal plan: lunar fast food (relative term) and fine dining. Bringing us to the question of dessert, specifically chocolate, which would be of dearest interest to me. Well, cocoa trees can grow up to 40 feet tall, so they'd obviously have to be dwarfed, perhaps not a top priority. But in that case there might be a workaround. As we saw, 3D printing has an assured future on the moon as a way to build things. Printing food doesn't work as well—it comes out as glop—but glop is fine for chocolate. In fact a Japanese company right now will sell you 3D printer "chocolates" made from hydrocolloids and shaped like the head of your sweetheart.

That sold me. The moment I heard that, there I was: kicked back in the herbarium, sucking on the ever-softening lump of my lover and making a meal of the stars.

CHAPTER 5 NOTES

66   **much larger size on the Moon:** "William Herschel and Trees on the Moon," Dr. Beachcombing's Bizarre History Blog (May 23, 2011), http://www.strange history.net/2011/05/23/william-herschel-and-trees-on -the-moon/.

     every imaginable production of a bounteous soil: *New York Sun* (August 25–31, 1835). "A smaller red fruit, shaped like a cucumber . . . was also lying in heaps in the center of several of the festive groups; but the only use they appeared to make of it was sucking its juice, after rolling it between the palms of their hands and nibbling off an end."

67   *poof, poof, poof*—**flowers and fruit:** For some reason this sparked an orgy in the play. See: "At the Theatre de la Gaite: *Le voyage dans la lune*," as reprinted in the *South Australian Advertiser* (March 29, 1876).

     raging vitality of its plants: Elizabeth Smith, "Is There Life on the Moon?," *Astronomical Society of Pomona College* 7, no. 2 (April 1922).

     Ants in a Field of Wheat: "Moon Men 750 Feet Tall!," *Fort Wayne Journal-Gazette*, Fort Wayne, Indiana (February 12, 1922).

68   **Onions would produce sprouts 33 feet long:** Albert Parry, "Soviet Cities on the Moon?," *Science Digest* (February 1958).

69   **gigantic cabbages, carrots and apples:** *New York Times* (March 14, 1956).

70   **Re: health benefits of algae:** "Spirulina," University of Maryland Medical Center, http://www.umm.edu/health /medical/altmed/supplement/spirulina.

Vitameatavegamin: It never gets old. "Lucy Does a TV Commercial" (sadly paid, still worth it):

https://www.youtube.com/watch?v=6T8bLJ4FqeU

The algae, in turn, will become food for the crew: Michael A. Tribe et al., *Ecological Principles* (Cambridge University Press, 1975).

horns and offal through the closed system: Ibid. To Dr. Robert Tischer, a microbiologist at Mississippi State University, the perfect creature to take along would be a "dwarf ruminant, probably the size of a cat, which had no

hoofs, claws, hair, horns etc. [and] which could be eaten in its entirety."

71 **serious yields of frosty buds:** "Hydro report: grow without soil bigger better buds," *High Times* (2013). Hydroponics isn't necessarily the only way to go. The Obayashi Corporation of Japan hopes to create lunar farms with enriched regolith feeding up to 10,000 people.

72 **the vegetables look weird:** Gioia Massa, author interview.
pretty dwarf and very productive: Ibid.
Re: 660-pound chicken: Mark Schatzker, *The Dorito Effect* (Simon & Schuster, 2015). The origin of this drive can be traced back to the 1948 Chicken of Tomorrow Contest.
Svalbard Global Seed Vault: The need for it is no longer theoretical. See Gul Tuysuz and Arwa Damon, "Arctic 'Doomsday Vault' opens to retrieve vital seeds for Syria." *CNN* (October 19, 2015). However, the unanticipated rush of climate change now threatens the vault. In May 2017 it was breached when meltwater from warming permafrost flooded the entrance tunnel.
reduced to eating their dead: Tony Williams, *The Jamestown Experiment* (Sourcebooks, 2011).

73 *gouamba,* **meaning "meat hunger":** A.J. Liebling, "The Great Gouamba," *New Yorker* (December 7, 1946).
Re: number of cells in the body: "How Many Cells Are in the Human Body?", https://wonderopolis.org/wonder/how-many-cells-are-in-the-human-body.
coaxed into steaks and chops: Foreshadowed in William Gibson's totemic sci-fi novel *Neuromancer.*
built by a Dutch team: Maggie Fox, "Lab-grown meat is here—but will vegetarians eat it?," *NBC News* (August 5, 2013). To be specific, it was made with "engineered muscle stem cells grown in a broth from a calf blood product." Ironically, as a New York rabbi has pointed out, this "cruelty-free meat" won't be kosher unless the cells are taken from a ritually slaughtered animal.

cow in a column: "Cow in a Column? A Synthetic Food Replicator Project," (July 8, 2015), https://catalog.data.gov /dataset/cow-in-a-column-a-synthetic-food-replicator -project.

74 "reliable declines" in the food value: "Dirt Poor: Have Fruits and Vegetables Become Less Nutritious?," *Scientific American*, May 2011.

75 Re: 250+ non-organic additives in organic food: Stephanie Strom, "Has 'Organic' Been Oversized?," *New York Times* (July 7, 2012).

gorgeous Audubon-type pictures of plants: Some of Mariah Wright's foods of the future can be viewed here: http://cargocollective.com/mariahwright/CROP-CO NSTRUCTS

beam their logos onto a full moon: Steven Kurutz, "Moonvertising," *New York Times* (December 12, 2008).

If the moon naturally, coincidentally had a Pizza Hut logo: Felix Salmon, "Great hypotheticals of our time," (October 11, 2006), http://www.economonitor.com/ana lysts/2006/10/11/great-hypotheticals-of-our-time/.

Domino's Pizza Japan projecting the cost: Julian Ryall, "Domino's Plans Pizza on the Moon," *Daily Telegraph* (January 9, 2011).

76 3D printer "chocolates": Nate Lanxon, "Japanese Café Produces Chocolate Version of Your Head for Valentine's Day," *WIRED UK* (January 25, 2013). Also: Daniel L. Cohen et al., "Hydrocolloid Printing: A Novel Platform for Customized Food Production," *Procedia Manufacturing* 1 (2015): 308–319.

CHAPTER 6

SEX

So far sex on the moon has played out only in the theater of the mind, but the critics are raving. "The very act of making love on the Moon will last much longer," warbles "British sex expert" Dr. Andrew Stanway, since "every lover will automatically be six times lighter," every movement six times etc. etc. In that precious bit of gravity lies the difference between rocket sex and lunar sex, which futurist Adrian Berry too sees as "one of the great joys of the 21st century."

Lovely as that is to imagine—and by all means wander that paragraph at your leisure—we have no actual evidence to prove it. Lunar sex looks fabulous on paper, but that's all we know. For now the closest we can come is to cross the lunar road to another theater where a sort of companion piece is up and running. Some bulbs are out in the marquee and the lobby's trashed, but the entertainment never stops. You've

probably starred in it yourself. Welcome to jealousy, faith-lessness, heartbreak and revenge.

Put sex off-world, and all the rest will come right with it. Do you doubt it? Picture yourself on the moon. Take all the ruinous romantic mistakes you've ever made and your instinct to repeat them, deposit them in a landscape bleak and strange where your need is enormous and the talent pool minute. *Res ipsa loquitur.* Warnings of fraught liaisons on long space flights to come are almost common coin in psy-chiatric journals, but the moon will offer a far bigger field of action: panoramas of geek noir played out in a shadow-land of obsession and love gone wrong.

Maybe nothing can prevent it. I have though come across one proposal to ease the pressure up there, which is that set-tlers could marry robots.

Some innovations I can be slow to like. In fact, the pull of technology can often be measured by the lines of my heel marks along the road. It's a prejudice, and I'm aware of it. So I've given myself every possible chance to warm to this idea, and it still creeps me out on so many levels I don't know where to start. Assuming it could really happen, which is the first question of course. Could robots and romance conceiv-ably mix? Could it be that a technology that traces its origins back to Jacques de Vaucanson's mechanical defecating duck of 1739 . . .

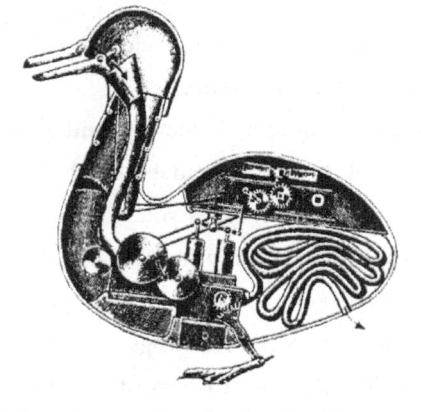

. . . really hold out hope of everlasting love?

Actually, to be ruthlessly honest, that's not the first question. If we're talking about having sex with a robot, as one would expect in a marriage, the first question that zooms through my brain, subliminally almost, leaving behind vapor trails of revulsion is: How lifelike are we talking? On a granular level what's in the pants? It's not easy for me to type that, let alone ponder it. Then again it might matter less than I think. According to Andy Clark, author of *Natural-Born Cyborgs*, marriageable robots won't just look and sound like people—the *Blade Runner* template—but we'll also be banging them with great good will because our brains "are primed to seek and consummate . . . intimate relations with nonbiological resources." That may say more about Mr. Clark than it does about you or me, but if he's right, it would help a lot.

Of this much I'm certain: if a moon colonist goes this route, he/she will have to bring a lot to the party. That's what

drives the inflatables market: the buyer brings the dream. Not a very elevated dream, true, but it's turned a profit, and the earliest, most rudimentary sexbots will have to offer at least that. And they are! In 2010 TrueCompanion.com went live selling "the world's first sex robot," Roxxxy, in a choice of six personalities, starting price $7,000. (According to designer Douglas Hines, his original plan was to create a working replica of a friend who died in Tower One of the World Trade Center, but "after test-marketing, the concept changed in order to capitalize on the enormous adult-entertainment industry.") Roxxxy doesn't have to be sophisticated for many men to like her because, as Lenny Bruce observed, men will do it to mud, and also because men objectify women, virtually all women. We do. I do. On being first introduced to a woman my mind runs like this: smile, lightning take, crude, after which I engage on other levels more or less sincerely, but the lightning is bottled and stored. It can be stored up top or down deep, but it's there forever. Women, as far as I can tell, don't objectify all men. They objectify two men: the one with the oiled abs and the cowboy hat, and the one in the hunting jacket with the frothy shirt, and they objectify these same two men over and over again. I think a case could be made that of these different forms of objectification, the male and the female, the male's is the more generous and nuanced.

The point I'm tacking toward is that as long as hotness is all that counts, and the market confines itself to smart-dildos

and so forth, I can see how they could satisfy a legitimate need—and satisfy it brilliantly as they grow more advanced. Eventually, writes David Levy, author of *Love and Sex With Robots*, "The number of sexual acts and lovemaking positions commonly practiced between humans will be extended, as robots teach more than is in all of the world's published sex manuals combined." To me that sounds more alarming than attractive, but clearly it's a zillion-dollar business.

Loving a machine, however, and being loved in return is a different thing altogether, and there I see nothing ahead but grief.

First, manufacturing robots as emotional partners means programming male and female behavior and sending it on dates. Right away you've got a thousand issues. What's male and what's female? Who decides? Who writes the codes? The answer to each of these questions is a flaming pileup of science, sociology and politics. For years feminists have been demanding an equal role in designing cyborgs, laying siege to the man-wall of Silicon Valley because what we've seen of sexbots so far—overwhelmingly female, if by female we mean stunned by size of cock, servile, grateful, domineering on demand—is for the women's movement a distillate of all the baseness lurking in men. And the fight will only get tougher. Targeting bimbobots is fairly straightforward, but when the software gets more complex, the sexism will be harder to spot and easier to deny.

In that case, to pluck an idea from American jurisprudence, the remedy for bad bots is more bots. Women will have to fire up kilns of their own, and even then we're just beginning. Whither gay robots, transgender, the whole spectrum of being? If we can get past eldritch elements of touch and feel, twilight-zone pillow talk and the whole concept of synthetic intercourse generally, I have to believe the arc of fuckable robots will bend toward justice.

That leaves us with one more river to cross.

The last challenge is to move from dateable machines to creating personal life partners. How do we bridge this immensity? Well, futurists tell us that after the basic model is picked, the client could customize it. Customize how? One approach, they say, could be recreating a lost love.

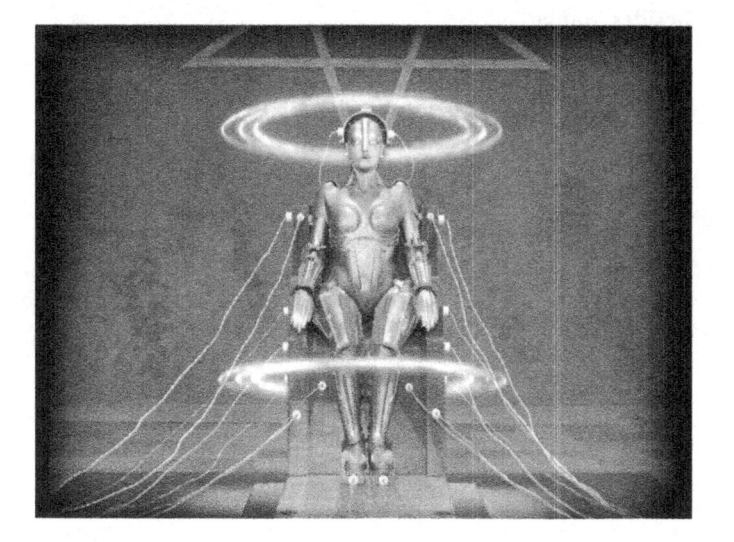

Imagine that! The yearning slaked, the ghost reoccupied, un-conflicted, *yours* . . . Just to feel the hope crack open, to how many of us does that speak? And easier surely than starting from scratch. There's a massive market here if it really works, price no object. You know it would sell. It's even been tried.

In 1912 a Viennese artist named Oskar Kokoschka be-gan a romance with the widow of Gustav Mahler. Her name was Alma, they came together like opposing weather fronts, and when they weren't fucking, he painted her. One day he was standing in her living room executing yet another por-trait, a mural over the fireplace, this one depicting her in a great fan of light and a likeness of himself, to one side, in hell surrounded by snakes. After watching him work for a time, Alma's small daughter piped up: "Can't you paint anything besides Mama?"

The artist wasn't alone in his ecstatic suffering. Two years later, near the breaking point, Alma wrote in her diary:

> *I must tear him out of my heart! The stake is embed-ded deep in my flesh . . . Away with him!—My nerves are shattered—my imagination ruined. What fiend sent him to me?*

When she swept out the door for good, Kokoschka was left in a state beyond description. Finally he gathered himself suffi-ciently to send a letter to a puppet-maker in Munich, Hermine

Moos. In it he commissioned her to create a life-size replica of Alma. For the next six months instructions poured from his pen:

> *Pay special attention to the dimensions of the head and neck, to the ribcage, the rump and the limbs . . . Please permit my sense of touch to take pleasure in those places where layers of fat or muscle suddenly give way to a sinewy covering of skin. For the first layer (inside) please use fine, curly horsehair . . .*
>
> *Can the mouth be opened? Are there teeth and a tongue inside? I hope so!*

In the meantime he busied himself preparing the house and buying her gowns and French underwear. At last the package arrived.

From the sinkhole of his disappointment he wrote to Frau Moos: "I was honestly shocked by your doll, which although I was prepared for a certain distance from reality, contradicts what I demanded of it and hoped of you in too many ways!" This so-called skin, for example, made her look like "a shaggy imitation of a bedside rug."

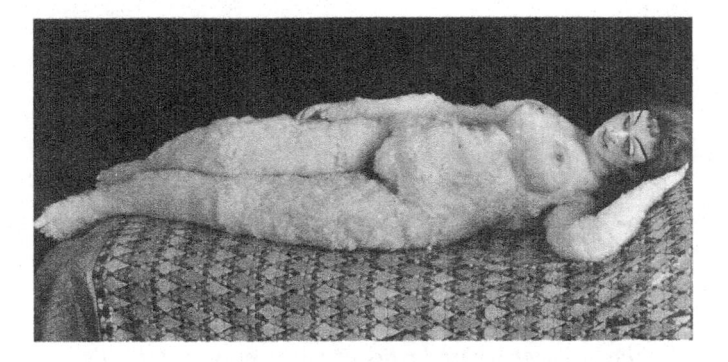

Kokoschka was bitter, he hated the doll . . . yet his eye kept returning to it. Soon he was wooing and whispering to his Other-Alma, as he called her. He even painted her portrait some thirty times. Eventually though, even he saw that the relationship was irretrievably one-sided. One evening he hosted a party at his atelier in Dresden. In the garden a chamber orchestra in formal dress filled the air with culture while Other-Alma in all her finery was paraded before the guests. Dinner followed, more wine than food, after which to shouts and applause he beheaded her in the backyard.

Let us now take this tortured lover and transport him to a spring morning some years from today. This time a different package arrives. He lifts Other-Alma out of the box. He follows the instructions to activate her, a little clumsy with excitement. Moments later there she stands, as perfect as a candle flame—inside as well as out, for thanks to the intricate customized software he knows her the moment she speaks.

How thrilled she is! How she's missed him! He takes her in his arms and they waltz the world away.

There's your core market. In the field of lost-love robotics there's no question that people like Kokoschka, both male and female, will be wildly satisfied customers. The problem, I would argue, is that a client base of stage-four lunatics will not be enough to sustain an industry of any size over the long haul. The less delusional the customer, the more discriminating he becomes. At its core it's an input problem. I don't see how any of us could bring enough to the software because we don't really carry the memory of the person we lost. We carry ten or twelve images and clips, memories replayed again and again both as was and as might have been if we'd had more luck or courage. In other words, one can't reasonably expect anything to grow green from exhausted soil and seeds fossilized by the grip of addiction. I rouse myself in the lab, I dig down for stories, memories, I go on and on like Spalding Gray till the techie's head is on the table and the results will still be the same. None of us knows another person, however er dear of heart, more than glancingly, through the cracked prism of our own minds, a philosophical truism I doubt will be in the brochures.

All right then, if lost love is a non-starter, perhaps creating a brand-new companion might work. Factory fresh! Packed with features! David Levy foresees a lavish catalogue of options like "artificial empathy" and "simulated religious pref-

erence," which the buyer could fine-tune at will. All right, let's think about that. You've bought, added, adjusted, tweaked; your new partner's personality is honed to perfection. Now let's say you've had a hard day. You come home cranky and aggrieved, after a couple of scotches you suspect you're not getting your bot's full attention so you find the remote. One click and you're getting more artificial empathy. But the next day it's annoying. Or let's say, tired of hearing about the Gaza Strip, you want to dial down its "simulated religious preference." The more choices one has, the more tempting it will be to add, subtract and change your mind until the whole thing ends in tears.

There's more. I haven't even touched on legal rights for robots, apparently coming (see endnotes), another mare's nest for domestic partnerships—*Wait a minute, I programmed you and you're taking me to court?*—and they especially won't work on the moon (to return there at last) where obstreperous software will be the last thing a tech-weary colonist will want to cope with.

Finally, no robot, however sweetly disposed, will be of help with the sine qua non on which lunar society will depend: propagation of the species. As it is, the whole area of having lunar babies is still a complete unknown, like almost everything else on the moon regarding the human body. On the most basic level, we don't know how much gravity is enough to stay healthy. (As NASA physician Jim Logan has said, "We

still do not have an inkling of what the 'gravity prescription' is. We don't know the dose, we don't know the frequency, we don't know the side effects.") Nor are we able to find out here because, at least so far, we can't create a stable, lighter gravity on Earth to run tests. We don't know how drugs will affect the body on the moon, even the simplest, or their impact over time on the heart and brain. Organs could swell, shrink or migrate. We don't know. We'll find out. There may be a run of funerals, but we'll learn.

As for reproduction on the moon, again we walk in darkness. Will men produce healthy sperm in one-sixth gravity, or women viable eggs? If you freeze and ship zygotes from Earth, could embryos successfully develop? Would a child on the moon become a physiological prisoner there?

I did have one thought about producing children on the moon. As an idea it's no great shakes, more of a last-resort thing, but as long as we're talking . . . In 2005 researchers at Cornell University announced the invention of robots that could both replicate themselves and disassemble each other. So here's what I'm thinking. First, you design a robot child to your dream specifications. Program it to build a slightly bigger version of itself every three months. Then the bigger dismantles the smaller and you sell it for parts.

CHAPTER 6 NOTES

82   **every lover will automatically be six times lighter:** As quoted in Adrian Berry, *The Next 500 Years: Life in the Coming Millennium* (W.H. Freeman & Co., 1996).

       one of the great joys of the 21st century: Ibid.

83   **common coin in psychiatric journals:** e.g., Kira Bacal, "Complicating Factors: Issues Relating to Romance and Reproduction During Space Missions," (January 2, 2009), http://www.medscape.com/viewarticle/585644. The topic is one of those clustering under the hot new rubric of astrosociology.

       de Vaucanson's mechanical defecating duck: Voltaire wrote that without the pooping duck "we would have nothing to remind us of the glory of France." But it had many admirers. In Thomas Pynchon's novel *Mason & Dixon* it has gained a beak of Swedish steel (*le Bec de la Mort*) and is trying to kill a chef.

84   **intimate relations with nonbiological resources:** Andy Clark, *Natural-Born Cyborgs: Minds, Technologies, and the Future of Human Intelligence* (Oxford University Press, 2004). To be fair, the idea has floated around for at least a hundred years. A German silent film featured a puppet-maker producing robots (before there was such a word) for "bachelors, widowers and misogynists." (*The Doll, [Die Puppe]*, Ernst Lubitsch, dir., 1919.) A good movie actually, inventive and sometimes beautiful: "*Die Puppe* (1919)": https://www.youtube.com/watch?v=hmAaO5i7DnE

85   **TrueCompanion.com went live:** http://www.truecompanion.com

       do it to mud: Lenny Bruce, *The Berkeley Concert* (1965).

86   **The number of sexual acts and lovemaking positions:** David Levy, *Love and Sex With Robots* (Harper Perennial, 2008).

feminists have been demanding an equal role in designing cyborgs: This campaign goes back at least as far as Donna Haraway, "A Cyborg Manifesto: Science, Technology and Socialist-Feminism in the Late Twentieth Century," in *Simians, Cyborgs and Women: The Reinvention of Nature* (Routledge, 1991). When couched in the language of higher learning—"biological-determinist ideology," "gender as performative," etc.—these polemics have a remarkable soporific force, but the justice of their thesis is unassailable.

89   *Are there teeth and a tongue inside?*: Nicholas Fox Weber, *The Bauhaus Group* (Yale University Press, 2011).

90   **beheaded her in the backyard:** The saga of this extraordinary romance is detailed in various articles and websites. See, e.g., www.alma-mahler.at/engl/almas_life/rese rl.html

91   **David Levy foresees a lavish catalogue of options:** David Levy, *Love and Sex With Robots* (Harper Perennial, 2008). The two I mention are found there.

simulated religious preference: A feature that should make the bot especially lifelike. Half the people I grew up with had simulated religious preferences.

legal rights for robots: "According to research commissioned by the United Kingdom Office of Science's Horizon Scanning Centre, robots could one day demand the same citizen's rights as humans": Alexander Bolonkin, *Universe, Human Immortality and Future Human Evaluation* (Elsevier, 2011). See also Robert Geraci, *Apocalyptic AI: Visions of Heaven in Robotics, Artificial Intelligence and Virtual Reality* (Oxford University Press, 2012).

92   **we don't know the side effects:** Alan Boyle, "Outer-Space Sex Carries Complications," *NBC News* (July 24, 2006).

93   **researchers at Cornell University:** "Self-Reproducing Robots Set to Push Boundaries of Space," (May 11, 2005), http://www.spacedaily.com/reports/SelfReproducing _Robots_Set_To_Push_Boundaries_Of_Space.html.

CHAPTER 7

WEALTH

Alfred Lord Tennyson had some thoughts on buying and selling in outer space. As he saw it, when "the heavens fill with commerce, argosies of magic sails / Pilots of the purple twilight dropping down with costly bales," universal peace would shower down as well. Today the future looks to some of us more like walking into a propeller, but not everyone agrees. Some have caught the opiate perfume of phrases like "Persian Gulf of the 21st century," "Saudi Arabia of platinum," and "greatest wealth-creation opportunity in modern history." They believe that new energy sources from the moon, non-polluting and inexhaustible, could transform and heal our planet. Equally excellent, they see themselves profiting unimaginably from these sources without interference or restraint.

Capitalism this pure, it's almost too good, it's like uncut heroin, it stops the breath. Look at the target market! Every-

body! Experts at MIT say the 10 billion people on Earth in 2050 will require seven to eight times the largely poisonous energy we're generating now, or would if they were still alive. The inexorable message: we've got to escape fossil fuels whatever it takes.

Truth to tell, there's so much talk about fossil fuels nowadays that the word *oil* makes me a little bit sleepy. So just a word or two on the subject and then we'll move along.

A couple of years ago I took a trip to a lower portion of the Arctic. Before I left, I was already planning my return—I would say to various women, "I'm just back from the Arctic," and they would say, "The Arctic! Wow!"—but as I trudged over iron ground through a wind causing me an almost religious form of suffering it seemed like a tough way to get laid. The locals weren't unhappy however. Quite the reverse: there in Churchill, Manitoba (pop. 923) on the edge of Hudson Bay, the creaking and cracking of harbor ice was coming earlier each year. Weary, stale, flat and unprofitable for centuries, Churchill seemed poised to make the leap from municipal amoeba to world hub. I stood on the wharf and imagined climate change arriving on the first oil tanker, coming down the gangplank waving and pointing at friends in the crowd.

That's the unimpeded future: we plunder the Arctic in the teeth of reason till the sun is a blot of ink and the world's remaining animals scurrying northward splash and sink in the chilly seas, all because of our relentless "addiction to oil."

Actually that's a lazy and inaccurate phrase. If it powered my car while getting me high, then I'd be addicted to oil. It's more like being trapped in the world's most abusive marriage. Counseling hasn't helped. We keep saying we want to break away, yet we remain economic and psychological hostages. Absent intervention I can see myself with absolute clarity standing with streaming eyes, blistered lungs and sea water up to my shins still filling the tank.

But I might not get the chance. Some think oil will abandon us.

I had a taste once of what that might be like. My family spent an oil-free winter when I was four. We were in Speedsville, New York, a town as small as me, living in a house the parish had donated to the new minister and his family. From the living room you could actually see little strips of the road through cracks in the wallboards, and the wind through the house was ridiculous, so I spent several months tottering about in my snowsuit indoors with the pee bucket frozen in the upstairs hall. Sometimes we'd sit in the car with the motor running.

But even then there was gas in the car. In the future that "peak oilers" see coming there won't be. There'll be no oil, period: when we've sucked up all we can feasibly reach, the power grids will implode. As the spirited Dimitry Orlov, a leading "doomer" puts it, world governments in league with "highly compensated senior lunch eaters" and "marionettes

controlled by giant bags of money" will produce a "super-power collapse soup . . . Make no mistake about it: this soup will be served, and it will not be tasty!" After that, doomers say, life will go on after a fashion: technology paralyzed, temperatures up, marauders on horseback and drifting curtains of swamp gas but a future still, a functioning society, or rather a lot of small societies like medieval towns but with a lot of marijuana. Survivalists, a rival tribe, have other ideas. When the sirens sound, the survivalist will reach for his BOB ("bug out bag") containing Swiss army knife, compact multi-function shovel, 5-in-1 whistle and N95 Respirator Dust Mask (box of twenty). Then it's off to his BOL ("bug out location") in his BOV. Or he might already be in his BOL as survivalist guru James Wesley Rawles was when he spoke with me by telephone from an undisclosed location ("My neighbors don't know I'm here."). Weathering the collapse of world order—less a question of if than when—will require, he said, a three-year food supply, a remote fortress and constant vigilance to keep out the "sheepies" who didn't prepare. What his own headquarters looks like he quite reasonably didn't share, but I've learned since that the Vauban Star, though pricey, is especially well regarded because of the opportunities it offers for lookout posts and crossfire:

Vauban Star
Credit: John Cote

Laid before us then are two opposing routes to TEOTWAW-KI: too many fossil fuels or not enough. Either way we're looking at decimation and death. Or are we? *Are these the shadows of things that will be, or are they shadows of things that may be, only?*

It's here that we slip into a river of dreams—realizable perhaps, I can't say otherwise—all set about with money trees. Small but mighty sectors of business and government see our salvation in a substance called Helium-3, an isotope of the party-balloon element. Earth has almost none because our magnetic field repels it, but the moon has enormous quantities hiding in the regolith—enough, we're told, to provide us all with 100% clean power into the far, far future. There could be 1 million tons for the scooping, and a mere 25 tons would fill America's energy needs for a year. (These are mad-libs numbers, the prospectus kind, but you get the idea.) The

web page "Helium-3 Moon/Celebs in Bikinis" only begins to suggest the level of interest. Russia's Energia Corporation has vowed "industrial-scale delivery" of He3 to Earth. The Chinese are determined to control it themselves. India, Japan and Germany want some. And Harrison Schmitt, the lone geologist to walk on the moon, has founded the Interlune Intermars Initiative to seize a bunch for the USA, which may explain why the Russians have accused us of plotting to corner the market and "put the rest of the world on its knees."

All this we find in the hymnals. Now for the obstacles, large and sobering. First, there's the task of putting specialists with vast equipment on the moon. Then there's digging, extracting and shipping the stuff. But most of all, there's the problem of what to do when it arrives here. For to be of any use, He3 has to spark with hydrogen in a fusion reactor at temperatures so high they would essentially melt the reactor, leaving us with a puddle of nothing. The container we need does not yet exist.

Thus for every He3 enthusiast you'll find someone who thinks it's a Fata Morgana that will only dissolve in our hands. Thus also the lively competing interest in putting solar panels on the moon instead. Solar energy! Like a big hug from Mom! Unless Mom is bitter and complicated, which is possible, given that the first attempt to use solar power in space was made by—who else?—the Nazis. When Allied forces stormed a German research lab in 1945 they found

sketches for a mammoth *Sonnengewehr*, or "Sun Gun." This was conceived as a giant sodium mirror which, orbiting 5,100 miles up, would harvest sunlight, tilt, point, and shoot lasers at Earth: death rays, in short. Today's Lunar Solar Project is approaching things from a friendlier angle. Led by physicist Dr. David Criswell, the LSP envisions powering Earth completely from the moon: laying the panels, setting the satellites, triangulating the beams and delivering the goods to an estimated 10,000 receiving stations craning for it like baby birds. It would be wildly expensive, the geopolitics is unimaginable, but the technology itself is well within reach. Of course, there's potential for abuse. At that level of accuracy an LSP worker on the moon sipping coffee could turn an ex-boyfriend into a pile of ash from a quarter million miles away. We should expect it to happen, in fact. It's like the NSA employees who've been busted for cyber-stalking their exes: honeycombs of power routinely offer dark chances to the rank and file.

I'm wondering now if I would incinerate an ex. What about you? It would be but the work of a moment. I suppose it depends on whether you nurse an eternal flame of resentment or sentimentalize the past and marinate in loss. Why pick one? You could run down the row . . .

But that's neither here nor there. If the core industry on the moon is producing energy for Earth, what other kinds of interchanges between the two can we expect to see?

First of all—to mark the negatives—lunar colonists will have to be on the qui vive against a lot of crap they don't want. By that I don't just mean the hail of urns, steel poems and so on arriving with the food and supplies. There will always be people on Earth eager to use the moon as a dumping ground. We've seen attempts already. When the federal government tagged Nevada's Yucca Mountain to receive 77,000 tons of spent plutonium, there were immediate cries to re-gift it to the moon. Research on lethal bacteria? Put it there. Criminally insane? Here's your ticket. Worst case, colonists may have to man the guns. Conversely, there's the issue of Earth trying to take stuff away. When trade begins, the imbalance will be near-total: Earth supplying A to Z while the moon replies with bottled water and crafts, but as time goes on . . . Actually if I were a settler, I'd even be cautious about giving my crazy senior partner a taste of that water. If all the desalinization plants chonking away from the Arctic to Argentina are being swallowed by rising tides, then somebody's going to take a hard look at the moon. Indeed, lunar water will be even more precious than first appears. H and O are the Fred and Ginger of elements; the routines they can perform together are dazzling and many; introduced by Edward Everett Horton (platinum), they even generate electricity, and the moon is full of platinum. Another twirl and they're rocket fuel! Now the moon is a "service station in the sky," a platform to Mars. Launches toward Earth won't need fuel at all. High-tech cata-

pults with payloads of titanium, aluminum, magnesium, etc. could be slinging it all back home. Possibly you're wondering why we have to go to all that trouble when the estimated value of metal particles in US sewage is $3,316,000,000. But some quests are more glamorous than others.

Meanwhile from lunar pole to pole people and goods are humming along on an infrastructure so cool, so technologically sexy, it will make America's roads, bridges and trains, already a global embarrassment, look more of a shambles than ever. Magnetic-levitation railroads (already running in Japan) are almost certain to appear, along with more conventional bullet trains (Japan, Europe, Uzbekistan [!]). Cable cars like ski lifts could be sliding along overhead. Plus whatever's running on the roads.

Roads are vital. Otherwise lunar vehicles struggling for traction will churn up a disastrous amount of dust and that killer static electricity. So yes, roads, made of volcanic glass, tougher than steel, thanks to manufacture in a vacuum.

As for what runs on them: frankly the traffic could be a bit scary.

Along the moon's highways vehicles are swooping and looping, some driven by people, some by robots. Not, however, all. Carnegie Mellon is among those working to create "telerobotic virtual experiences on the moon," which means people on Earth operating lunar vehicles by remote control. This sounds like a groove but for one thing: "We still haven't

figured out," a designer said, "how to address the light-travel time delay," meaning that those at the consoles would be driving a few seconds in the past.

How then to reduce the loss of life? One way could be an increased reliance on AGVs—Autonomous Ground Vehicles, i.e., driverless cars—a concept that as you know has already seized the headlines.

Here we have a peerless example of how fast technology can move. I happened to be present when driverless cars—or rather a bunch of gallant, struggling prototypes—first appeared in public en masse: in March 2004 outside the Slash X Café biker bar in southern California. The occasion was the DARPA Grand Challenge, a contest concocted by the Department of Defense, which offered a million-dollar prize to anyone who could build a vehicle that drove itself. On display were the fifteen finalists, spawn of grad-school departments, garage freaks, even a high-school team: re-wrought Hummers, pickups and the like cabalistically decorated and bristling with colored wires. The challenge: to negotiate, via software only, a twisting, 150-mile route through creosote and sagebrush ending at Buffalo Bill's Casino in Primm, Nevada.

So it's bone-cold dawn, and I'm sitting in metal bleachers, hunched, with twenty or thirty other interested parties, waiting. We're not alone. Beneath the chatter of Army helicopters there's a loose swarm of sheriff's deputies, state police, security guards and Bureau of Land Management agents, scores

of them, in addition to the eighty US Marines deployed along the trail. Some ways off I can see biologists on their hands and knees still putting pens around the wildlife.

Just then four Marines in full-dress uniform, two with enormous flags, appear across the way riding identical palominos. They come to a stop. A couple of generals on the announcer's platform remove their hats for a recording of "The Star Spangled Banner." Then comes a speech drowned by the choppers as the first contestant moves into view.

"We're 30 seconds from history!" cries the PA.

A man in a black-and-white referee shirt whips a green flag.

"Ladies and gentlemen, in chute five, Bob!"

Bob, originally a 1996 Chevy Tahoe, moves past us through the far gate and makes a magic left. Down the road it goes maybe fifty yards, then stops. Hundreds of hushed onlookers watch to see what Bob will do next. Nothing apparently, at least for now. So DAD, a computerized ex-pickup, gets the green flag. We watch DAD. DAD passes Bob.

An encouraging start, giving little hint of the carnage to come. In the next few minutes, No. 25 from Virginia Tech stops dead, smoking, and has to be shoved off. CajunBot expires against a rock. Something long and painted like an alligator lurches down a slope into a nest of barbed wire.

"Can you imagine the people in the Middle East seeing a bunch of these autonomous vehicles coming at them? They'd surrender without a fight!" the announcer cries, as No. 13

from Falls Church, Virginia, trundles past the grandstand and turns over on its side.

And so it goes. Since this isn't a Disney movie, the high-schoolers' entry collides with the first available wall. Ultimately Sandstorm, the Carnegie Mellon car, gets the farthest: 7.2 miles, or 5% of the route.

The next year, six vehicles make it the full 150 miles.

That's the speed of change. Nowadays we've got AGVs headed for the showroom, and by the time they reach the moon there's no telling what they'll do.

Unless they've been replaced.

In 1959 Hermann Oberth, one of rocketry's great pioneers, published sketches of a "Moon Car" with a leg. It looked like this:

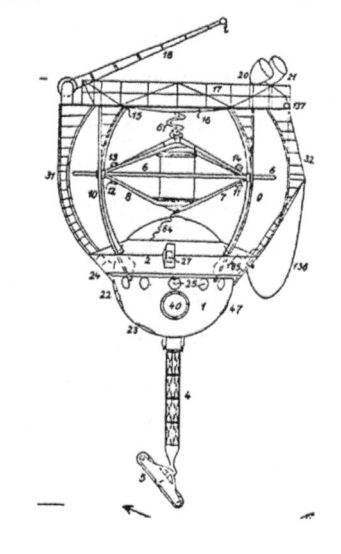

His idea was that astronauts riding inside could cross rough lunar terrain by hopping. The Moon Car drew scorn at the time, but the leg idea never quite died. It mutated, grew more legs and lives on today in robotics projects like the one at Case Western Reserve. The progress of the cockroach, it turns out, is the most sophisticated in nature: six active limbs simultaneously performing three distinct tasks. The rear legs drive it forward, the middle two turn and lift as it climbs, and the front legs act as sensors to find the next footholds, selecting from thousands of possible adjustments the very best. You'd think the sight of a huge artificial insect climbing out of a crater would scare the primal shit out of people. Nevertheless, a DARPA manager told me, since discovering the robo-roach, "we're not sure the wheel's the way to go."

CHAPTER 7 NOTES

97   **dropping down with costly bales:** Tennyson, "Locksley Hall," (1835).

Persian Gulf of the 21st century: Nick Davidson, "Making a mint out of the moon," BBC Horizon (April 9, 2007), among others.

Saudi Arabia of platinum: "Colonization of Space needs economic justification," (September 15, 2012), http://powerfromspace.blogspot.com/2012/09/colonization-of-space-needs-economic.html?q=colonization+of+space+needs+economic.

greatest wealth-creation opportunity in modern history: Barney Pell, co-founder and CTO of Moon Express, as quoted in Steve Robbins, "From FIRST Robotics to the Moon," (February 1, 2012), http://www.digitaleng.news/de/from-first-robotics-to-the-moon/.

98   **seven to eight times the largely poisonous energy we're generating now:** Daniel G. Nocera, "On the future of global energy," *Daedalus* 135, no. 4 (Fall 2006).

99   **peak oilers:** This faction dismisses "the mirage of alternative fuels." Clinical psychologist Dr. Kathy McMahon, a doomer herself, has coined the term "Panglossian disorder," which she defines as "a neurotic tendency toward extreme optimism in the face of likely cultural and planetary collapse." For more, including a fascinating look at the Scarlett O'Hara and Rhett Butler subtypes, see: "Do You Have a Panglossian Disorder?" (November 26, 2007), http://circleof13.blogspot.com/2007/11/do-you-have-panglossian-disorder.html

100   **it will not be tasty!:** Dmitry Orlov, *Reinventing Collapse* (New Society Publishers, 2011).

    with a lot of marijuana: Ben McGrath, "The Dystopians," *The New Yorker* (January 26, 2009).

    reach for his BOB: See, e.g., "Off-the-Shelf Bug-Out Bags Buyer's Guide," (December 29, 2015), www.offgridweb .com/gear/off-the-shelf-bug-out-bags/

    My neighbors don't know I'm here: James Wesley Rawles, author interview. To Rawles the end of oil isn't the only possible endgame. "An X-class solar flare could do it," he said. "The last one was in 1859 so that's becoming more likely. A hydrogen bomb set off at high altitude, even economic collapse could wipe out the grids."

    What his own headquarters looks like: A feature it almost certainly has is one he's famous for devising. The "crushroom" is a false entryway designed to entrap looters and supplicants. Depending on the threat level they can then be dealt any one of six levels of punishment.

    lookout posts and crossfire: Survivalists sometimes react to being called paranoiac like Bette Davis in *All About Eve* ("Paranoiac!"). Rawles told me that in large part that portrayal is a distortion by mainstream media, and he may be right. He sounds quite centered himself. All that said, for the most amazing example of applied paranoia I've ever seen check out "Constructing and Finding Hiding Pla ces, by Eli in the Southwest," https://survivalblog.com/con structing-and-finding-hiding-places-by-eli-in-the-south west/.

101   **100% clean power into the far, far future:** Numerous sources include Steve Dobransky, "Helium-3: The Future of Energy Security," *International Journal on World Peace* *30*, no. 1 (March 2013); Steve Almasy, "Could the moon provide clean energy for Earth?" CNN (July 21, 2011).

102 **industrial-scale delivery:** Adrian Blomfield, "Russians see moon plot in NASA plans," *The Telegraph* (January 5, 2007).

world on its knees: Ibid.

The container we need does not yet exist: "Possible Future Energy Sources," in *Alternative Energy*, 2nd ed., eds. K. Lee Lerner et al. (2012).

103 *Sonnengewehr,* **or "Sun Gun":** "Sun Gun," *Time* magazine (July 9, 1945).

Lunar Solar Project: Amanda Onion, "Physicist Wants to Harness Energy From the Moon," http://abcnews.go.co m/Technology/story?id=98024&page=1. Japan's Shimizu Corporation seeks to create a so-called Luna Ring, a belt of solar panels circling the moon's equator, growing stylishly in width from a few kilometers to 400.

busted for cyber-stalking their exes: John Ribeiro, "NSA admits employees spied on husbands, boyfriends and girlfriends," (September 27, 2013), http://www.pcworld.com /article/2050100/nsa-admits-employees-spied-on-loved -ones.html.

104 **77,000 tons of spent plutonium:** Leonard David, "Moon Eyed as Ultimate Waste Dump," (August 22, 2002), http:// www.rense.com/general28/monn.htm.

Criminally insane? Here's your ticket: This kind of off-loading was thought of long ago. In 1611 John Donne suggested imprisoning Jesuits on the moon.

my crazy senior partner a taste of that water: How crazy? Well, let's extrapolate from the present. See, e.g., the BBC's "California's Worst Drought in 1,200 Years in Pictures": http://www.bbc.com/news/world-us-canada-32150064

Fred and Ginger of elements: from the immortal *Swing Time* (1936): https://www.youtube.com/watch?v=mxPgpl MujzQ

the moon is full of platinum: For more on hydrogen-cell technology as a third clean power source see Dennis Wingo, *Moonrush* (Apogee Books, 2004).

platform to Mars: The moon's greatest advantage as a launch site is how little fuel the rockets need: 1/5th the escape velocity of Earth TIMES 1/6th gravity EQUALS 30 times less energy needed to blast off. Thus the Houston outfit that will shoot your DNA into space for possible cloning by aliens, if they can someday shift operations to the moon, the benefit to their bottom line will be substantial.

High-tech catapults: known in the trade as "momentum exchange tethers."

105 **estimated value of metal particles in US sewage:** *Harper's* Index (June 2015).

Re: America's decrepit infrastructure: Elizabeth Drew, "A Country Breaking Down," *New York Review of Books* (February 25, 2016).

Magnetic-levitation railroads: David Schrunk et al., *The Moon: Resources, Future Development and Settlement* (Praxis, 2007).

roads, made of volcanic glass: Paul D. Spudis, "Regolith, the 'Other' Lunar Resource," (January 5, 2011), http://www.airspacemag.com/daily-planet/regolith-the-other-lunar-resource-156943194/.

some driven by people, some by robots: One of my favorite breakthroughs: Takayuki Kanda et al., "A humanoid robot that pretends to listen to route guidance from a human," *Autonomous Robots* 22, no. 1 (January 2007).

106 **driving a few seconds in the past:** "Virtual moon trip coming up," (June 1, 2007), http://www.nbcnews.com/science/cosmic-log.

DARPA Grand Challenge: This section is adapted from an article I wrote for the London *Sunday Times Magazine*, "The Mechanical Army," (May 23, 2004).

108 **sketches of a "Moon Car" with a leg:** Hermann Oberth, *The Moon Car* (Harper & Brothers, 1959). For a lavish parade of visuals—every moon vehicle ever thought up and then some—see "Ground Cars and Flitters": www.projec trho.com/public_html/rocket/flitters.php

109 **wheel's the way to go:** Author interview.

CHAPTER 8

THE DOOMSDAY ARK AND THE
ALIEN PRIEST

Space travel is a theology that needs no god. Some find one anyway—moonwalker Charles Duke returned from his trip a born-again Christian—but the presence of great wells of faith in something out there, something infinitely discoverable, doesn't mean there has to be a king of it. In this religion, science and dreams finger outward to the very rim of possibility, the Cheshire Cat and Schrodinger's romp together, and the worshipper's one desire is the chance to play too.

So it is with the moon: beyond the solutions to food and shelter, beyond the practicalities of trade, all brilliant enough, a nimbus of the marvelous rings the whole, hints of dreams beyond the obvious. One of these, barely crystallized yet, takes our survival instinct and beams it through a sort of giant prism. As we've seen here on Earth, bunkers are proliferating as we speak (did I mention doomsdaydwellings.com?). We've got our Norwegian seed vault. We've got a "charitable

frozen zoo project" in Britain storing DNA samples of endangered species. We've got Vivos Cryovault (not a charity) filing sperm and eggs so that post-Armageddon your grandiose genes can help repopulate the planet. But all of them are candles in the wind compared to the lunar Doomsday Ark.

Maybe you picture at first, as I did, a hulk and a ladder and no one about, but this is not on its face a nutball scheme like some. Conceived by the NYU-based Alliance to Rescue Civilization, the Ark project would begin with burying "all human knowledge" on hard discs on the moon. In the event of a global disaster, this information would be transmitted in six major languages to "4,000 heavily fortified radio receivers stationed on Earth" so that those left moaning in the rubble would have the blueprints to rebuild. But that's nothing really, that's the prosaic part, for as Bernard Foing of the ESA, a champion of the project, described it to me, this "lunar lifeboat" would be more than a library, more than a DNA bank: it would be a breeding site as well. So for example if we killed off Earth's last giraffe, new ones could ship from the stock already on display in lunar zoos. "In the long term," he said, "you could re-create whales. And then later, when we build whole biospheres on the moon, we could have lunar seas for our whales to swim in."

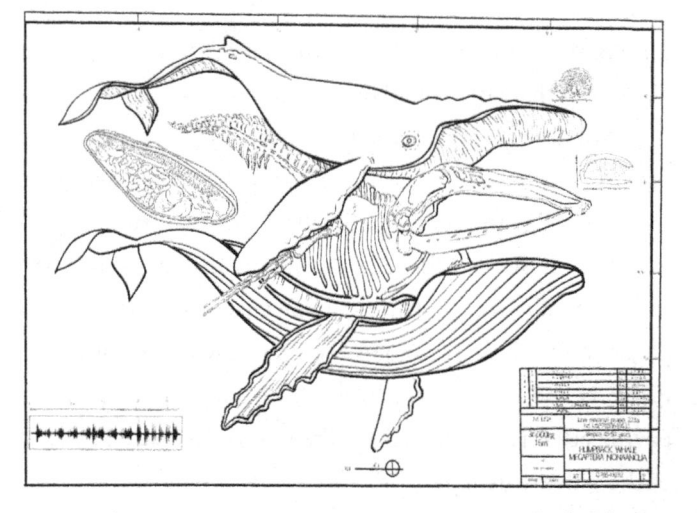

Credit: John Cote

Theoretically I get what he's saying—well no, I don't, but I'm willing to believe it's possible. The hardest part, it seems to me, lies in re-creating a good first whale. In 2010 dart-gun samples from 955 whales found "high levels of cadmium, aluminum, chromium, lead, silver, mercury and titanium" in virtually every one. "You could make a fairly tight argument," said the project chief, that ocean contaminants represent "the single greatest health threat that has ever faced the human species," and as for whales themselves, "I don't see any future . . . except extinction." So you see the challenge. With a prognosis like that, if we're going to have a whale we can work with, we'll have to get the lead out as it were. It would be bad

for morale to ship toxic DNA to the moon, grow new whales and watch them die out all over again.

Hard-core skeptics of the Doomsday Ark see a more basic flaw. It goes back to those radio signals sending Earthward the knowledge to regrow civilization: how will survivors (if any) find those receiving stations (if any left) and utilize the information (with what?)? But I don't see why that's so complicated. People on the moon could fly down with coffee and blankets and explain it to them. If people on the moon are paying attention, that is, if they're not too drunk on the rest of the universe to care.

Let's turn with a breath of relief to something unambiguously positive: the Hubble telescope. For almost thirty years it has been sailing through space to the strains of *Blue Danube Waltz*, a contender for the best thing science ever built. It has peered 10–15 billion light years into the past. It has revealed to us 10,000 galaxies, each spilling billions of stars. Yet all this overpowering wonder is a teaser, a mere bagatelle, for strategically pitched on the moon—no electromagnetic din to fret them, no pollutants, in the purest peace—comparable telescopes could see 100,000 times farther. And those telescopes would not be comparable. They would be far, far better: spinning liquid mirrors, we're told, built on-site in lunar foundries, "telescope farms," scores of them—Argus peering into the soul of time. Then, one astronomer says, "It will be possible to obtain highly detailed images of the most distant

objects in the universe." Well, probably not, but that's how excited he is.

The risk here (there's always a risk) is that peering so deeply into the universe, though salutary in small doses, could be incapacitating in large, putting one's ego into a sort of existential cyclotron. There will be times I expect when colonists will have to creep away and recover their reason with something like hunting for aliens.

Aliens we're used to. Klaatu! ET! The Glob That Girdled the Globe! There are as many different kinds as there are people to imagine them although only a few of us know where they are. (*Thank you for signing the petition asking the Obama Administration to acknowledge an extraterrestrial presence here on Earth.*) What's more, as the search escalates here—in 2016 Chinese bulldozers displaced thousands in Guizhou Province to make way for a new tracking station—top-tier scouts are already calling dibs on prime spots on the moon. The venerable SETI Institute in California is eyeing Daedalus, a crater on the edge of the dark side protected by peaks, where it hopes to install a giant radio telescope. Just about everyone in the business dreams of a lunar outpost, especially lately. Since the 1990s the minds of astronomers have been boggled and re-boggled by the discovery of billions of planets orbiting remote suns. The more suns, the more planets, the more likely life—including that grail of grails, "life as we know it."

I have to say that finding "life as we know it" strikes me as a pretty weird goal. Haven't we had a bellyful of life as we know it? Given our luck with it, isn't finding more the last thing we should want? We should be hoping for something as different as possible, though I realize of course we can't choose what we discover. *How* we look for it, that we could control, but there's even a fight about that. On one side are those who simply want to monitor outer space: Fuddlike we should be very, very quiet and just listen. They are opposed by the braver or cockier "pingers," who favor shooting out signals seeking a reply, a strategy the first group regards as "dangerous, bordering on suicidal." An unimaginable something somewhere hears a sound, then another. Ponderously it opens its eyes . . .

But then it has to get here. How is the question.

The fact is, if we should rouse intelligent life, it will more likely be able to communicate than visit. That sounds perfect to me. We could swivel slowly in our chairs, playing with rubber bands and swapping stories with these creatures instead of slaughtering or enslaving each other. What put me in mind of this—communicating at a comfortable distance—was an item I came across about attempts to talk to aliens during the Civil War. It's a little murky how it all started, but according to Charles Fort, an early 20th-century author and assiduous compiler of paranormal lore, there occurred in the early 1860s a sudden interest in what looked like activity on the

moon. Apparently some Americans took it to be a response to the turmoil of battle along the eastern seaboard: they thought moon dwellers had mistaken it as an attempt to attract their attention, and that as a result "the Chiaroscuroans, or the lunar communicationists, [seeking] to be intelligible to this earth by means of lights and shades," had gathered near the Sea of Tranquility and were forming "changing compositions . . . some of them dressed in white and standing in a border, and some of them dressed in black . . . all of them unified in a hope of conveying an impression of the geometric, as the product of design." Eager to reply, groups of Americans "arranged themselves in living patterns: flags, crosses, and in one instance, in which thousands were engaged, in the representation of an enormous Liberty Bell." Charles Fort was not an infallible historian, and I have searched in vain for confirmation that these particular demonstrations took place—and yet: the June 1866 issue of *Harper's* magazine carried a report that a group of astronomers had laid out slabs of stone representing the Pythagorean theorem in hopes that "lunarians" would reciprocate with a mathematical formula of their own, an effort swiftly followed by other proposals for contacting alien life such as assembling the world's navies in a big circle to flash their searchlights or turning London's flaring gas supply on and off to represent notes of music. So there was something in the air.

At any rate, I like the long-distance template for talking to aliens, although to be honest safety is not my sole concern. I'm also reluctant to meet ETs because of my status as an introvert.

Rebecca West once wrote of "the grey ice that forms on an Englishman's face as he is introduced to a stranger." What produces it in the English I couldn't say, but it's a coating I'm familiar with. There's no major anxiety attached, just an instinct that talking to this new person will be work.

Like many others, I discovered what introversion was on the killing ground of summer camp. Each morning began with the ritual shout for blood—

> *Strawberry shortcake*
> Huckleberry pie
> H-Y-D-E B-A-Y . . .
> Are we in it?
> Well, I guess
> Hyde Bay, Hyde Bay,
> Yes! Yes! Yes!

—during which those such as myself (still chanting) calculated the day ahead, long hours of wan jealousy and futile watchfulness which were teaching me something fundamental about who's who in life and what's what. Ironically perhaps, if aliens had appeared there some quiet evening on the

shore, with the sailboats lapping at their buoys and the lake offering its tray of light to the moon, we might have gotten on quite well drawn together in a spirit of fellow feeling. But if they showed up on Earth today someplace lurid like Times Square, then soldiers and the media would rush to surround them and we introverts, frightened or not, would get shoved to the back.

Whereas, if they call but don't come, we can all get to know them.

This isn't the kind of thing most people worry about, I know. It's the boutique concern of a certain kind of neurotic. So let's move on to something of more moment to more people, namely, how ETs might affect organized religion.

Given the papacy's historical attitude toward astronomers (*Release the hounds!*), I have to say today's Catholic Church seems remarkably broadminded on this score. The chief of the Vatican Observatory has said he's ready to welcome any "brother extraterrestrials," and the Vatican itself has hosted two inclusive conferences on the likelihood of ETs and how the church might respond if they washed up here. Actually the question has been raised before. In the 17th century the German philosopher Gottfried Leibniz mused: "If someone came from the moon, we might grant him the title of man but when it came to baptism there might be great disputes . . . I doubt whether he would ever be acceptable as a priest in the Catholic Church because, until there was some revelation,

the consecration would always be suspect." Yet his pondering tone suggests that the idea of ordaining aliens is still worth discussing—something women have yet to achieve—and the modern Church dismisses his qualms. (*"Meet the pope's astronomer, who says he'd baptize an alien given the chance."*)

Most faiths, it turns out, incorporate the possibility of other life: Hindu, Moslem, Jewish, Mormon. The only sector wholly unnerved at the prospect appears to be Christian fundamentalists. As the Atlanta head of Creation Ministries put it, "My theological perspective is that ET life would actually make a mockery of the very reason Christ came to die for our sins." But I think I've found a way to relieve his mind. I came across it on a website called "Roman Catholic Replies," hosted by ultra-conservatives of that faith ("truly Catholic" as opposed to "what the Modernists pawn off as Catholic"), a group much in tune with their Protestant counterparts. An article posted there reports an incident in which a Brazilian was abducted by a UFO. Awakening to find himself stretched on a table, the victim "was able, with great effort, to reach into his pocket. He found his rosary and pulled it out and began praying loudly the Hail Mary. At that moment the aliens looked at him with anger and said, 'Now you've spoiled everything.'" And they took him back.

Why would alien kidnappers be thwarted by the rosary? The answer of course is that they wouldn't be—thus proving, the article explains, that these creatures weren't aliens at all

but agents of Satan in disguise, "demons playing their usual games with ignorant humans. What better way to deceive modern man than through the science he worships?"

Many evangelicals believe in a similar "hierarchy of demons" out to ensnare us. In other words, if they're putting on costumes, the cosmos remains intact.

In this ocean of unknowing one other possibility remains: that aliens exist but we'll never find them. Hugo de Garis, an AI expert based in China, has a provocative take on this notion based on his interest in "femtotech." This is theoretical technology at the level of 10 to the minus 15th meters, with a processing power a trillion times a trillion times greater than nanotech. Should a life form latch onto that, it could *reduce* its presence, growing mightier and mightier and smaller and smaller, virtually to the vanishing point. In that case we'd be Horton trying to hear the Who without the means to do it.

Or maybe it's very much simpler than that, the reason behind the great silence so far. Maybe aliens have approached us intending to visit, discovered that the ring around our planet is a wheel of garbage, and gone back home. Either they couldn't get through, or it looked to them like one of those front yards with the rusted-out cab of a pickup in it and trash and a cow's skull and an overturned refrigerator in the weeds, and one of them said, "I don't know about you, but I'm not ringing the bell," and off they went. If that's true, if the aliens out there have crossed us off entirely, then we lonely campers

on the moon—and we'll all be lonely, every one—straining to make contact, yearning for friends, will be in for a long, doomed vigil, reduced at last to a void of our own making.

If so, however, we still have the Great Consoler.

All the gold on Earth, all the iron, platinum, nickel, you name it, came from the wreckage of asteroids, and right now 9,000 more are tracing orbits not far away. We're the fox, they are the grapes, and we want them, but unlike the fable these are grapes we could reach by launching from the moon. What's more, by analyzing the light they reflect, we can figure out ahead of time the best ones to shoot for. Near-Earth Object 3554 Amun, for instance, contains about $8 trillion worth of nickel and iron, $6 trillion in cobalt and $6 trillion in platinum-group metals.

In 2012 came word of an even bigger discovery, the Diamond Planet. Formally known as "55 Cancri e," it has an estimated worth of $26.9 nonillion.

But we're getting ahead of ourselves.

CHAPTER 8 NOTES

115 **charitable frozen zoo project:** Otherwise known as the Frozen Ark, its long-range hope is to clone back into existence creatures we force out of it.

116 **Vivos Cryovault:** For much more in this vein ("Join Us at the Largest Survival Community on Earth!") see: http://www.terravivos.com. The ambition of this scheme was briefly dwarfed by the Million Dollar Time Capsule (reddit/r/shittykickstarters).

lunar lifeboat: Dr. Foing, author interview.

lunar seas for our whales to swim in: Bernard Foing, "Noah's Ark on the Moon," *Astrobiology Magazine* (February 27, 2006). The term "Doomsday Ark" has been applied fleetingly to other things as well. During a panic in China in 2012 triggered by the Mayan prediction of the apocalypse, rumors flew that arks had been built in the Tibetan mountains and that the United Nations was selling tickets.

117 **I don't see any future . . . except extinction:** Arthur Max, "Toxins Found in Whales Bode Ill for Humans," *Associated Press* (June 25, 2010).

118 **see 100,000 times further:** http://www.adrianberry.net. Site is down at this writing.

most distant objects in the universe: David Schrunk et al., *The Moon: Resources, Future Development and Settlement* (Praxis, 2007).

119 **The Glob That Girdled the Globe!:** This was the working title for *The Blob* (1958), starring Steve McQueen. Notable for the meta-brilliance of its attack on teenagers in a movie theater. Clip here: https://www.youtube.com/watch?v=GODDLgM1gKo

Chinese bulldozers displaced thousands: Edward Wong, "China Telescope to Displace 9,000 Villagers in Hunt for Extraterrestrials," *New York Times* (February 17, 2016).

Daedalus, a crater on the edge of the dark side: Paul Gilster, "Protecting the Lunar Farside," *Centauri Dreams* (June 18, 2010).

the discovery of billions of planets orbiting remote suns: Joel Achenbach, "NASA estimates 1 billion 'Earths' in our galaxy alone," *Washington Post* (July 24, 2015). An old idea whose time has come. In the 17th century, a period of wide speculation on the "plurality of worlds," René Descartes suggested that every star could be a potential sun surrounded by planets.

120 **dangerous, bordering on suicidal:** Marc Kaufman, *First Contact: Scientific Breakthroughs in the Hunt for Life Beyond Earth* (Simon and Schuster, 2012). Stephen Hawking is among those concerned that ETs "may not see us as any more valuable than we see bacteria."

121 **representation of an enormous Liberty Bell:** "Marchers on the Moon," (June 14, 2010), http://www.airspace mag.com/daily-planet/regolith-the-other-lunar-re source-156943194/.

slabs of stone representing the Pythagorean theorem: Henry Draper, "Are There Other Inhabited Worlds?," *Harper's* (June 1866).

to represent notes of music: "Contacting Mars in the Late Nineteenth Century," (May 25, 2015), http://www .strangehistory.net/2015/05/25/contacting-mars-in-the -late-nineteenth-century/.

122 **as he is introduced to a stranger:** Rebecca West, *Black Lamb and Grey Falcon: A Journey Through Yugoslavia* (Viking, 1941).

123 **brother extraterrestrials:** "Vatican astronomer cites possibility of extraterrestrial 'brothers,'" *New York Times* (May 14, 2008).

Vatican itself has hosted two inclusive conferences: Nicholos Wethington, "Vatican Holds Conference on Extraterrestrial Life," (December 24, 2015), https://www.universetoday.com/44713/vatican-holds-conference-on-extraterrestrial-life/. Also: Megan Gannon, "Is Alien Life Out There? Vatican Observatory Co-Hosts Conference in Southern Arizona," (March 16, 2014), https://www.space.com/25060-vatican-observatory-alien-life-conference.html.

the German philosopher Gottfried Leibniz mused: As quoted in: "But Could ET Believe in God?," *Sunday Telegraph* (April 2, 1997).

124 *baptize an alien given the chance*: David Gibson, "Meet the pope's astronomer, who says he'd baptize an alien if given the chance," *Religion News Service* (December 3, 2014).

a mockery of the very reason Christ came: Marc Kaufman, "The religious questions raised by aliens," *Washington Post* (November 8, 2009).

125 **than through the science he worships?:** "UFO's, Extraterrestrials and the Catholic Church," http://www.roman-catholic.com/Roman/Articles/ufo%27s.htm.

a trillion times a trillion times greater than nanotech: Paul Gilster, "SETI at the Particle Level," *Centauri Dreams* (February 12, 2014).

126 **$6 trillion in platinum-group metals:** "Space Settlements spreading life throughout the solar system," *NASA Ames Research Center*, http://www.nss.org/settlement/nasa/index.html.

In the space-MMO game EVE Online, asteroid mining is popular "due to its simplicity," but in reality it will be something of a chore. First, there's catching the asteroid. This will most likely involve overtaking it from behind, drawing alongside rodeo-style, then snagging it via magnet, hook or harpoon; next, winching oneself toward it by

cable. . . . Or one could harness the asteroid by deflecting its orbit via nuclear bomb, kinetic impactor (impulsive), gravity tractor, mass driver, pulsed laser etc., any of which sounds irresponsible and indeed presents two immediate threats, collision with Earth (unintentional) and collision with Earth (intentional), for its potential use as weaponry (fuck the money) is part of its allure.

$26.9 nonillion: Andrew Fazekas, "Diamond Planet Found—Part of a 'Whole New Class'?" *National Geographic News* (October 13, 2012).

CHAPTER 9

FUN

In years to come, as rockets crammed with earthlings come streaming toward the moon, the difference between holidaymaking and mass exodus will have to be nicely judged. There are getaways and getaways, and our lunar colonists will have to keep a weather eye out if they want to prevent being overrun.

But let's say for the sake of argument that there's no near-term stampede. Let's say Earth somehow lurches along riddled with illness, a fabulous invalid like the theater. In that case there'll be a line out the door at Silver Sickle Vacations.

How the concept got started you'll read in the brochure, so let me just summarize. In the 1920s, when paying customers were first cruising about in planes, the next leap of the mind was naturally putting them in space. There followed a raft of theories on how to do it, from experts, the lightly qualified and the loons, all covered with more or less equal

optimism in the press since they sounded equally farfetched. A Princeton physics professor foresaw a spaceship 110 feet in diameter with "a dozen or more cannons" firing from its sides, sufficient to send a raft of passengers on a two-month cruise to the moon and back. Why not? The man was a registered egghead. Didn't Einstein work at Princeton? In the spring of 1927 the *New York Times* ran a feature about Russian plans to capture the moon-tour market led by one Ivan Fedorof of the All-Inventors' Vegetarian Club of Interplanetary Cosmopolitans, "with several thousand members, using a new language based on five vowels and five mathematical signs . . .

"[Fedorof] says that he will fly to the moon in September in an apparatus called a 'rocket,' 30 meters long, half airplane and half giant projectile. . . . After flying as an airplane to a height of 15 kilometers, the 'moon machine' will fold its wings, simultaneously exploding a terrific mixture of three secret gases in lateral cylinders opening toward the tail," a self-relieving burst of such force as to drive it all the way to the moon. There the crew equipped with "novel respirators" would collect new gases "rendered breathable by a special plant," thus allowing sufficient time to construct a terminus for a "future line of aerobuses." To the degree that this scheme depended on secret gases, novel respirators and a special plant, there was room to doubt it. However, Germany's premier rocket scientist, Max Valier, was said to be making the

trip and, the *Times* also reported, the renowned Prof. Robert Goddard was conducting research along parallel lines.

Such was the state of play in the 1920s. Vault forward nearly a century to the present, and what do we find? Mass-transit plans for outer space announced, canceled, re-announced and abandoned in half a dozen major nations while the Isle of Man, eager to shake its reputation as "70,000 alcoholics clinging to a rock," aggressively courts the space industry with tax breaks. The projected costs and profits involved in lunar transportation are a pillar of cloud. In other words, although plans for things to do *on* the moon are in reach, or nearly, getting people there in bulk is still a crusher unless the space elevator works.

Perhaps that's overstating the case—I would expect some raucous jitneys to be running by then—but the fact remains that the hot science in moon transit has coalesced around a vertical railroad made of "buckyballs" rising 62,000 miles into the sky. "Buckyballs," named for Buckminster Fuller, are carbon nanotubes of recent discovery; inside a dizzying shell of them passengers would ascend in a car along a thin diamond wire to a sort of platform . . . You know, I'll just pass this from my imagination to yours. The point is that in the very long run the elevator would be safer and cheaper than a bunch of launches.

At the top, passengers would change to moon taxis for the rest of the trip.

The usual corporate monoliths are behind this project, but it hardly signifies; the elevator is so much pixie dust to me. However, as the tour groups arrive—the moon at last!—I suddenly see it all perfectly. I can see myself, part of the herd reeling from the ride as we're funneled through passport control. I see the armed immigration officers stationed in booths or lurking in offices, hosing up baksheesh, beating undesirables down with paperwork, letting the toothsome through in exchange for sexual favors—just another day on the distant edge of civilization—till at last, clutching what's left of our belongings, we reach the parking lot and the shuttles that will take us to our hotels.

These will be of two types: orbital and stationary. The orbitals will be an eye-popping extension of the Carnival Cruise model. That's the kind of hotel X-prize winner Burt Rutan wants to build, one that circles the moon glass-bottomed-boat style. ("You can do an elliptical orbit and miss it by ten feet if you want.") Another—but this one you know all about. You've experienced it: "Hilton Space Station Number Five" from Stanley Kubrick's *2001*.

Since that brilliant bit of product placement, Hilton's ambitions have shifted onto the moon itself. And the design, from British architect Peter Inston, they claim is good to go: a vast titanium rotunda enclosing 5,000 rooms with a supplementary "activity dome" and two towers. Once again, there I am with my group in our optional weighted boots as we

move in and out of the restaurants, the "Galaxy Lounge" and the chapel. Buses carry us to "lunar picnics" beside artificial lagoons. I'm peering into one now at the trout and tilapia, at the ribbons of algae caught by the starlight. I get a text across my eyes: *Lunchtime!* We settle ourselves, open our picnic baskets . . .

As big as he dreamed, one thing Mr. Hilton got very wrong was the probable quality of the food. He had no idea I'd be peeling back that snowy napkin to reveal items as succulent as they are strange. He thought, quite naturally, in the antique future of his time: "Today a four-ounce hamburger can be reduced to 1/5 ounce; a steak to the size of a silver dollar. When reconstituted, these foods will be as tasty and nourishing as any served on Earth." Drinks at the bar, he believed, would be on the Tang model: push a button and "out will come a pre-measured, pre-cooled mixture of pure ethyl alcohol and distilled water. . . . Into the mixture the bartender drops a tablet—martini, Manhattan, scotch, gin—you name it. Instant drink!"

Geh. Still, Mr. Hilton does allude there to the critical matter of staffing. Who will these lunar bartenders be? The cooks, the maids, the croupiers, where will they come from? They'll come from the University of Delaware according to UD Prof. Fred DeMicco, a leading apostle of "outer space as a new frontier for hospitality and tourism." They'll come from Georgetown University, from the Rochester Institute of Technology,

from perhaps (whispers here) Italy . . . a whole line of servants there to greet you in the driveway like on PBS. And yet, and yet . . . Don't you need a touch of Cathy or Heathcliff in your soul to go to the moon at all? I can't see someone spirited enough to make the trip donning a clip-on tie and little red vest when he gets there. (*Hey you, polishing the snifters. What are you really up to?*)

At any rate, that's the Hilton, our case study. When we iris out to take in the full range of lunar hospitality we find—Las Vegas! No, really, that's the goal. "It'll be like Las Vegas," Bernard Foing told me, "each hotel a fabulous, self-contained world completely disconnected from the environment." I sat with architect Hans-Jurgen Rombaut in a Dutch café as he spread out plans for what he called a "sensation engine," a lunar resort where guests would stay in teardrop-shaped "habitation capsules" in constant vertical motion, set in two glittering slanted towers offering views of other guests indoor-mountaineering or coasting about like bats. It's much the same at Escargot City, the Nishimatsu Corp. complex of three ten-story units shaped like snail shells—inside, a perpetual brain-pummeling present and outside, yes, "Las Vegas–style flashing neon signs . . ."

Casino gambling will be fantastically popular, Prof. DeMicco believes. But of course! Anyone who makes it to the moon will be a born gambler, every act charged with the question, *Do I feel lucky?* Settlers already accustomed to the

moon will probably strategize pretty well, but addled tourists not so much. Besides, they'll be lashed along by the entertainment which we can be fairly sure, whether it's drilling their eyeballs full-on or dazzling their peripheral vision or simply feeding every corpuscle by its very presence, will lean heavily on sports.

Here on Earth, if you were to jump straight up with your legs together, you'd spend about 0.7 seconds in the air. Do the same thing on the moon and you'd stay up 3.5 seconds. Now let's extrapolate from that. Let's take for example a simple game like E. M. Forster's bumble puppy, which consists of "striking tennis balls high into the air, so that they fall over the net and immoderately bounce." Fun on Earth maybe; fantastic on the moon, especially for kids. Now open the whole big box of sports. Place them on the moon one by one. What we immediately see is that minor ones on Earth become the top attractions. Look what happens to:

Diving
Gymnastics
Bungee Jumping OMG

Even at the blackjack table, hesitating over my king and seven, I'm aware that the pole vaulter overhead is sailing a country mile. One bounce on her trampoline and a showgirl vanishes; two hands later she's performing a Bob Fosse routine on the

way down. Add white tigers (reconstituted), crushing percussion and the leers of the victors, and I depart the temporal realm as completely as the dead.

Eventually of course it all becomes pole dancing. Hotels are not where lunar sports will really shine. For that, to see them (in the snoozy language of commerce) becoming "key media and financial drivers as the space experience economy grows," we have to look elsewhere—to a venue like the Orbital Sports Stadium (US/Japan), a giant arena housed in a rotating shell. Here's where the diving and gymnastics come to glory. Here's where swimmers propel themselves in and out of the water like flying fish. Here's where professionals will compete for cash and prizes, or so I assume since the design for this revolving stadium includes plans for 360-degree holographic commercials that would wrap around fans like pythons. And from there it's on to the real money, *LIVE FROM THE MOON,* beaming games to the dumbfounded back on Earth.

"It will change our culture," a bedazzled commentator writes. "It will change our dreams."

Not all sports will thrive so. Basketball would be unrecognizable. It would have to be played on floor, walls and ceiling with baskets 60 feet high, and dribbling would be out of the question. But baseball, that most elastic of sports, presents a more interesting case. Consider this:

A few years back a Brooklyn astronomy teacher named Peter Brancazio did a sort of Bill Jamesian micro-study of lunar baseball. What struck him right away was the loss of the Bernoulli Effect: curveballs, sliders, anything thrown with overspin to break downward would lose 5/6ths of their bite. Backspin, however, is another story. Pitcher to batter, it would produce "rising fastballs" that really rise. Even better, "a fly ball struck with enough backspin will rise and do a loop-de-loop before proceeding into the outfield."

That's the coolest thing since Ray Milland and his bat-repelling methylethylpropylbutyl, and I'd pay plenty to see it. It's not a game I'd play though. You see, according to Mr. Brancazio's calculations, a ball hit at an angle of 40 degrees on Earth and traveling 385 feet would stay in the air for 5 seconds whereas on the moon it would travel 890 feet and stay aloft 21.1 seconds. "This raises interesting questions," Mr. Brancazio said. "Where do you put the fences?" Personally I don't care about that. I'm too busy imagining myself as the outfielder under the ball. The extra hang time would not, as I thought at first, increase my chances of dropping it by 400%. It would be many multiples of that. In Little League I remember that unique anxiety, how it swooped, up and fast, till it suddenly reached a kind of sparkly place where no birds sang. *It's coming down.*

Credit: John Cote

Pro sports notwithstanding, everyone on the moon will have to exercise. Given the deleterious effects of prolonged gravity loss, even the laziest colonists will be hopping on and off treadmills and somersaulting along back lanes to keep their muscles from withering like winter apples. However ineptly, the tourist will have to do the same to keep his blood from pooling.

But a steely breed of holidaymaker will go far beyond that. These are the toned and prepped "extreme lunar tourists" upon whom hopes of fat profits are fixed. They'll be drawn to the moon by its bizarre new challenges: by the "cliffs that

rise sheer for thousands of meters," in promo language, "can-yons that twist for many a kilometer before disappearing into huge tunnels, and several mountain ranges, two of which, the Leibniz and the Doerfel, have peaks that rival the Hi-malayas." The climbing, the mountain biking, the bragging rights—nothing without the occasional corpse—will all feed the thrill.

Bringing us at last to day's end (though in the perpetual twilight it will be hard to tell). Whether one has spent the hours struggling up the Liebnitz, skidding a bike along the trails or, like myself, shuffling along a pressurized walkway past the Sea of Tranquility (Lunar Development Corp.), it will be time to return to the hotel and . . .

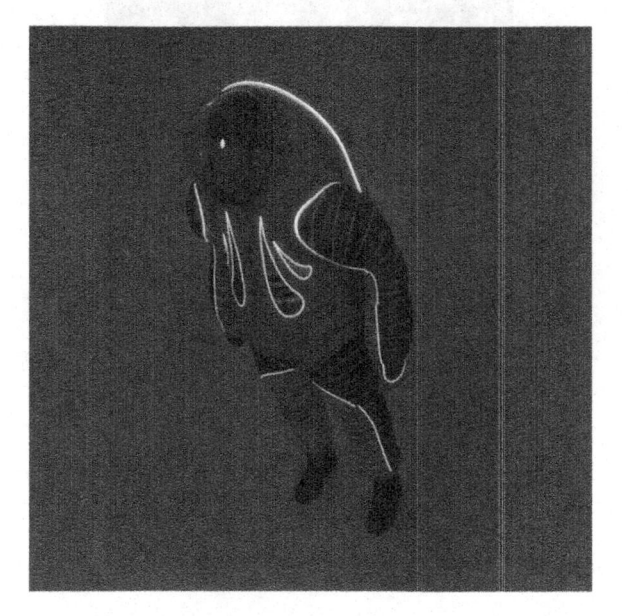

. . . get ready to party! When it comes to nightclubbing, these hot new looks are Vegas-ready, and NASA knows it:

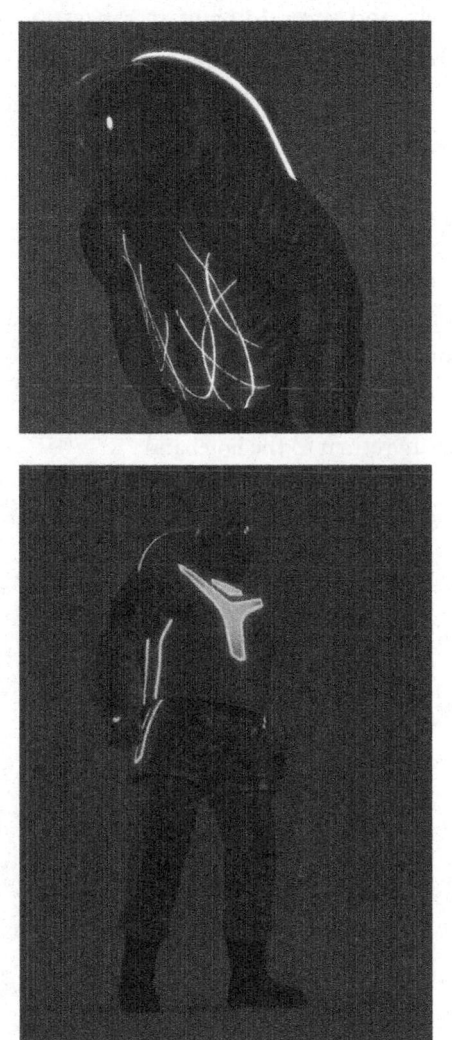

Its designers at the Advanced Concepts Lab even speak catwalk:

> *With its glowing natural lines shining against an all-black background, 'Biomimicry' aims to capture the deep-sea style of bioluminescent creatures such as the clusterwink snail, vampire squid and atolla jellyfish...*

Publicly the agency claims these suits will help moon workers "identify each other while mining for super-precious minerals," but we know they'll really be code in the clubs—the colors, designs, pulses, signaling who's into what—until suddenly the heart jumps:

"High-bouncing lover, I must have you!"

CHAPTER 9 NOTES

132 **a two-month cruise to the moon and back:** "Scientist Visions Trips to Moon by Year 2050 in Rocket Ships Making 50,000 Miles an Hour," *New York Times* (April 12, 1930).

renowned Prof. Robert Goddard was conducting research on parallel lines: "Plans Hop to Moon in a Rocket-Plane," *New York Times* (May 8, 1927).

133 **70,000 alcoholics clinging to a rock:** Lester Haines, "Isle of Man to Become 'Switzerland of Space'," *The Register* (January 25, 2006).

unless the space elevator works: "Nova scienceNOW | A Nanotube Space Elevator," *PBS* (August 26, 2008).

134 **miss it by ten feet if you want:** for more see Burt Rutan's TED talk, "The Real Future of Space Exploration": https://www.youtube.com/watch?v=nwfSENkvJXY

from Stanley Kubrick's *2001*: Looking at it again, I just realized the moon is rotating behind the guy's head: "*2001* Videophone Sequence": https://www.youtube.com/watch?v=vWwo6JpMceg

Re: Peter Inston's Lunar Hilton designs: "First on the Moon for the Hilton," *The Space Place*, http://www.resonancepub.com/space.htm. Also Judy Dash, "Great views and very little gravity," *Baltimore Sun* (January 2, 2000) and elsewhere.

135 **trout and tilapia:** These are the two fish I've seen mentioned as most likely to be farmed on the moon, tilapia in particular. ("They're the goats of the fish world," Gioia Massa said.)

Instant drink!: For the complete text of Barron Hilton's 1967 remarks, see "Hotels in Space": www.spacefuture.com/archive/hotels_in_space.shtml

outer space as a new frontier for hospitality and tourism: This is in fact the title of an article co-authored by Prof. DeMicco for *Hospitality Educator.*

136 **completely disconnected from the environment:** Bernard Foing, author interview.

sensation engine: Rombaut's concept appears as one in a series of "Top 10 Futuristic Hotels." Irrelevant but trippy: www.wonderslist.com/top-10-futuristic-concept-hotels

Las Vegas–style flashing neon signs: John Carlin, "Fly me to the moon," *The Independent* (March 7, 1998). The rivalrous Shimizu Corp. hopes to fill the Copernicus Crater with luxury condos. But these are technically residential.

137 **you'd stay up 3.5 seconds:** Ken Murphy, "Rollerblading on the Moon," (May 3, 2008), http://www.outofthecradle.net/archives/2007/01/t-1-day-and-counting/.

E. M. Forster's bumble puppy: as described in *Howard's End.* Not to be confused with Aldous Huxley's Centrifugal Bumble-puppy (*Brave New World*).

a Bob Fosse routine on the way down: With luck something along these lines: "Clip—Cell Block Tango (2002)": https://www.youtube.com/watch?v=TYmMagkfjfI

138 **as the space experience economy grows:** Katie Amey, "Orbital Cruise Ships . . .," *Daily Mail* (April 28, 2015).

Orbital Sports Stadium: Pierluigi Polignano, "New Frontiers of Tourism: The Extraterrestrial Space," (October 6, 2010), https://www.ramkshrestha.wordpress.com.

a bedazzled commentator: Robin Kool in the comments section of John Tierney's article, "Is the Moon Dull? . . .," *New York Times* (September 27, 2007).

Re: moon baseball: Bruce Weber, "If Baseball Expands to the Moon, Be Sure to Back Up Those Fences," *New York Times* (April 28, 2001).

139 **Ray Milland and his bat-repelling methylethylpropy-butyl:** From the movie *It Happens Every Spring* (1949). Chemistry professor Milland accidentally discovers a substance that repels wood. He coats baseballs with it and goes on to a big career in the majors. Presented as light comedy, the movie demonstrates how cheaters prosper.

141 **peaks that rival the Himalayas:** Adrian Berry, *The Next 500 Years: Life in the Coming Millennium* (Book Guild Publishing, 2015).

shuffling along a pressurized walkway: Jim Wilson, "Postcards from the Moon," *Popular Mechanics* (June 2000).

142 **these hot new looks are Vegas-ready:** Lenny Pierce, "Space Fashion: NASA's Latest Styles in the Astro Apparel of Tomorrow," http://nerdist.com/space-fashion-nasas-latest-styles-in-the-astro-apparel-of-tomorrow/.

143 **vampire squid and atolla jellyfish:** *Rolling Stone* writer Matt Taibbi once described Goldman Sachs, the world's largest investment bank, as "a great vampire squid wrapped around the face of humanity, relentlessly jamming its blood funnel into anything that smells like money," but here we're thinking more of a party animal.

CHAPTER 10

TROUBLESHOOTING

In the 1880s Oscar Wilde made a tour of the American South. He was there in part to promote a traveling production of Gilbert and Sullivan's *Patience,* a show in which he was heavily mocked. So he was bathed in even more irony than usual, but as he soon discovered, the beauty of it was lost on many still kicking through the ashes of their late crusade. Wherever he went, he later said, whatever he remarked upon, people told him, "You should have seen it before the War." Still, he never grasped the depth of feeling behind those words until the evening in Charleston when he said, "How beautiful the moon is!" Came the reply: "You should have seen it, sir, before the War."

In some stereopticon of the future I see a twist on that same idea: Earth's last survivors standing in their steaming rags looking skyward as reports of war are coming in.

I'll never look at it the same way again.

That's what they said when Apollo landed.
This is different.

Of course things may not play out that way. To say that once humans are installed on the moon, animosities may be provoked, insults traded, supplies sabotaged, systems hacked, caves bombed, shrines defiled and settlements leveled under cover of darkness is not to predict it. Peace, as I said before, could hold for quite some time. The problems of motion, everyone shifting about in a sort of burglar's creep, the care required for the smallest tasks, the thousand traceries of science connecting the whole: an awareness of living in a glass menagerie may be the very thing that protects it.

I'm less confident of that though after stumbling across a letter Leonardo da Vinci wrote in the 1480s. It turns out that technology's visionary supreme, the patron saint of the patent office, believed that ultimately nothing we invent will defeat the beast that stalks us from within. He pictured doomsday as the moment when the darkness inside all of us emerges and coalesces into one lumbering giant, and then "for us wretched mortals there avails not any flight, since this monster when advancing slowly far exceeds the speed of the swiftest courser . . ." Actually that scenario sounds a lot like *Forbidden Planet* (1956), in which Dr. Morbius (Walter Pidgeon) runs technology that once belonged to a vanished race—vanished, we learn, because they were attacked and massacred by their own "monsters of the id." But it's

one thing to watch Walter Pidgeon's subconscious running around loose. It's something else to come upon da Vinci describing the few survivors of the Great Suicide living "after the manner of crabs and crickets." At least it gave me pause.

Then I thought, Hell, I'm more optimistic than that.

But why? How can that be possible?

There followed a long spell of looking for hope with a flashlight. I knew it was there; I could hear it somewhere ahead beating around like a bat. But it wouldn't come near. So I gave up and whistled and thought of other things, and at last a couple of possibilities crept lichen-like to mind. The thing with feathers springs eternal? Yes, probably true and not to be sneezed at. The hope of a parent? That certainly. That's centered in my chest: it's the one kind of hope I think that grows stronger the worse things get. And there's a third thing too that cheers me. As anyone who watched thousands of hours of TV in the 50s and 60s can tell you, the idea of good guys clobbering bad guys enters the very marrow of the partially developed mind, and nothing that happens in later life ever completely expels it. Having been reared in this cult—for that's what it was, a sort of Procter & Gamble fundamentalism—in some faint, lambent way I'm still impervious to reality.

All together that's not a lot to push on with, but it's something—and who knows, as we think our way through man's

long-term lunar prospects perhaps we'll find more cause for optimism yet.

Let's start then with our mission statement: to live in peace on the moon. What's the chief threat? Sooner or later, "a gold rush with all the problems that entails," as astronomer Paul Spudis put it to me. On the moon the timeline might stretch like taffy, but ultimately human beings are what they are.

At least for now.

And here we must finally and fully confront the great question which has brooded over our lunar ambitions from page one. Will people who settle the moon be people as we now understand the term?

Human nature has always been, to take Harold Pinter's phrase, the weasel under the cocktail cabinet. Often we seem to ruin faster than we build. It's not inconceivable then that the long-term survival of our species may require changing the species. I'm just spitballing here; as far as I can tell that's not the motive of the people who are trying to do it right now. Really there is no motive, just a few zealots lashed to the next big thing. Modifying humans is doable maybe, therefore cool, and for good or ill the hapless rest of us will be dragged along behind the van. It's been this way forever. Take the airplane. The flying machine was not something that sprang into being, like the printing press or a cure for smallpox, out of an urgent common need. There were no crowds with torches demanding it. The percentage of us who, left unmolested, would ever

try to rise into the air is practically zero. But a tiny few were obsessed by it, they wouldn't let it go, and now here we are, all of us, at 30,000 feet, slaves to an industry deaf to rage and impervious to ridicule.

In the same way, certain elements now believe they can pluck the notion of the perfectibility of man out of the 18th century, turn it into hardware and project it to the stars.

Are they right?

In life generally the line between fact and nonsense is rarely clear. They're like next-door neighbors running back and forth between each other's houses. So when I read that future tech will transform the human brain from a scoop of ice cream into a banana split, that it will replace our bones with carbon-titanium and scrub our bloodstreams with nanobots until we achieve what's known in the trade as "effective immortality," I go blank. What am I trying to imagine? It's not like "picture yourself in an Oldsmobile"; it can't be done. So I simply don't know what to think. I look toward California and see champions of the cause like the president of Singularity University, Peter Diamandis (declared goal to live 700 years) and Ray Kurzweil, director of engineering at Google ("Death: I don't accept it")—a man known for popping 250 nutritional supplements a day (see endnote for complete list)—and I think, well, the obvious. Then I remember that people in direst need of therapy often make the biggest splash.

Actually creating better humans has been a dream since the dawn of the space program. Before astronauts took off at all, science was scouring the globe for ways to upgrade them. How did Tibetan lamas retain normal skin temperatures in subzero cold? How did Peruvian Indians labor in the Andes in such thin air? Answer such questions, one expert said, and "we can go to the engineers and say, 'Throw away half those oxygen cylinders. Our astronaut breathes like a Peruvian.'" These ambitions seem crude today. Now outside of Peru itself few care how or if they're breathing because tomorrow's advanced human won't depend on original parts but on fusion, an ecstatic union of the born and the built. And even that might be just a place to water the horses. This, according to Kurzweil, is how Optiman will be brought to climax: our newly synthetic beings will combine and recombine, moving platform by platform through the stars as we convert celestial bodies into computer substrate until finally, he says, "the universe is saturated with our intelligence," and we fuse into one vast computronium blazing as one light. Some in the AI field regard that vision as the equivalent of Cary Grant on LSD ("I imagined myself as a giant penis launching off from Earth like a spaceship"). They don't think AI can come anywhere near that. "You could have all the computer chips ever in the world," says neuroscientist Miguel Nicolelis, "and you won't create a consciousness." Others view the Singularity as patchy science at best or, to whatever degree achievable, the tenth

circle of hell. Elon Musk and Bill Gates are both frightened of artificial intelligence, or claim to be. "If I had to guess at what our biggest existential threat is, it's probably that," said Musk at MIT. "I'm increasingly inclined to think that . . . with artificial intelligence we are summoning the demon." Asked why if he's so afraid of AI he's a major investor in it—in Deep-Mind (owned by Google) and Vicarious, "a company aiming to build a computer that can think like a person, with a neural network capable of replicating the part of the brain that controls vision, body movement and language"—Musk said that he became a player "not from the standpoint of actually trying to make any investment return . . . I just like to keep an eye on what's going on." To me that's rather like a planter of the Old South saying, "I'm investing in slavery to keep an eye on it," but then Bill Gates is doing the same kind of thing. Maybe their inveighing and investing is protecting us in some complex way we have yet to understand.

As for myself, though as an English major my grasp of the Singularity is limited—in fact, the more I study it, the more opaque it becomes—on a subject so vast even those of us least equipped to voice an opinion may perhaps have useful thoughts. So here's what I know in my bones.

In all the talk about the prospects of transhumanism at whatever stage, about this fusing of man and machine—thrilling perhaps, or loathsome and tragic, your call—the debate is always over the science involved, the bullet train

of the possible. In these plans the social sciences aren't much involved and the humanities never. In short, there's precious little thought being given to human nature and its endless capacity for interfering with itself. The opportunities in this line are infinite. Moreover, roboticizing ourselves wholesale would involve innumerable steps, altering humans by degrees. Think for a moment how liquid we are. We're aquariums of thought and feeling; none of us is the same person for two hours together. Insert chips, and we become exponentially more different still. And where goes common purpose then? What about panic buying among the elite? Even before it's commercially available Augmented Cognition will be shooting out the back door to senators, CEOs, drug lords, terrified of being left behind. Otherwise, aside from a few geeks and balloon-heads it's the old normal for the rest of us until one day the stuff is out, like Ebola or crystal meth, it's everywhere. Now your dog walker is 6% AI or 28%. If I were offered the stuff myself, I'd turn it down flat. I've read *Portrait of the Artist as a Young Man* twice, I'd say, and acted in a lot of plays; I'm not tampering with my gemlike flame. Especially if there were reports by then of the law of unintended consequences or "revenge effects" among the 1%. But with more and more people using, at some point I might cave, that blessed feeling we artistic types have (or to be more precise, that delusion of being secretly envied) giving way to old fears from the playground. (*Don't pick me last!*) So I might go ahead and have

one small thing installed for fellowship's sake: say, a chip to make me financially responsible. That's it, no more.

Forgetting about the butterfly effect.

So now who is everybody? Because we're not talking anymore about us and them, people vs. robots. We're a whole continuum of beings shading from organic to synthetic and back again—much like the state of gender today which, as we're now discovering, consists of M and F and a universe between. In the same way, as they ring changes on the 86 billion neurons of the brain, humbots may self-identify in any number of ways. The great difference will be the unpredictability and speed of their shifts along the spectrum. And as long as human nature is leaking through the vents, anything can happen.

How all this volatility might affect our chances of peace on the moon I leave to you. As for the disputes themselves, the most likely flashpoints of war will be control of Helium-3 and/or the New Jerusalem of the south pole, but anything's possible. Actually it's sort of a weird rush, isn't it, picturing all those creatures us and post-us arrayed as if on the fields of Troy? Everyone armed with the very latest. Not that I'd want to be part of it. Had I the misfortune to be there I'd be stuffing myself like a goose with technology getting ready for the fight.

Then at last, stoked, armed and armored, I would emerge from my lunar cave and vanish in a puff.

For when war comes, the moon will be brilliantly ready, the equivalent of a ripe peach. According to a Congressional report called *Military Space Forces: The Next 50 Years*, it is "a nearly perfect environment" for laser weapons of whatever type (gas, chemical, solid state, etc.) because "light propagates unimpeded in a vacuum" producing a more penetrating burn. Likewise the moon will provide "a superlative environment" for chemical and biological weapons: "Clandestine operatives could dispense lethal or incapacitating CW/BW agents rapidly and uniformly through enemy facilities . . ." Nuclear weapons? Bring them on. Their deployment will be more artful and precise than here (unless combatants use way too many and blow up the moon altogether, sending Earth into an unpopular 3,000-mph spin: see Chapter 2), the reason being that in the lunar vacuum the range of fireballs will max out at about 65 miles. Even handguns will work. The Congressional report somewhat shortchanges this approach, but they could be of enormous use. A firearm, as the name implies, requires oxygen, which the moon lacks, but a normal cartridge comes complete with bullet, powder and oxidizer inside. The impact of the hammer sparks the shot. Lockheed used to run ads comparing the moon to the Wild West. A metaphor no longer! Real gunfights! Except all the math will change.

1. Thanks to lunar gravity the bullet would travel six times farther but not faster.

2. The speed required to put a bullet in lunar orbit is about 3,750 mph. A shot like that would add an extra fillip of danger since, as a Brown University professor points out, "theoretically you could shoot yourself in the back."

Credit: John Cote

3. The moon's escape velocity—the speed required to leave its gravitational field—is about 5,300 mph. When guns can shoot bullets that fast (not possible yet but soon), the ones that don't hit things will keep right on going and fly through space forever.

Throw in light-gravity tanks, Claymore mines, those nano-bots in the bloodstream (allowing hacking on a cellular level) and clouds of electrified dust zapping people like bugs in the backyard and you've got mayhem absolute. Long-lasting too: lunar foxholes will shield people better than on Earth because, as mentioned, a void shrinks the effects of blasts, and thousands of caves will mean lots of places to hide. Thus ragtag groups of guerrillas, DPs and wounded tourists can squirrel themselves away while outside the remaining warriors are dodging from rock to rock.

Around the blast zones some survivors are trying to escape: dragging out the tether launchers, grabbing plants from nurseries to throw aboard, the stronger helping the weaker onto the ships . . .

Reaching Mars will demand a lot: a 140-million-mile trip lasting several months at least, "even with the help of advanced—and as yet nonexistent—propulsion systems." But 3-2-1 and off they go, trusting in cold sleep, nutrient drips and muscle toning by robot slaves to get them through. Hoping as well not to run into any of the thousands if not millions of bullets with which the universe is now laced.

Perhaps they take a last look back at the moon's acres of carnage that could lie uneroded for thousands of years. Not necessarily the last word: other beings could try again.

In the early twenty-first century scientists found microbial life in South Africa's gold mines, the deepest pits in the

world. Ferocious bacteria eating sulfur and excreting hydro-gen sulfide have survived scalding heat and pitch darkness for some 40 million years. So the tenacity of living organisms is really amazing.

And where there's life, there's hope.

CHAPTER 10 NOTES

147   **seen it, sir, before the War:** Richard Ellmann, *Oscar Wilde* (Vintage, 1988).

148   **the speed of the swiftest courser:** as quoted in Lewis Mumford, "The Premonitions of Leonardo da Vinci," *New York Review of Books* (December 29, 1966).

      monsters of the id: A beloved sci-fi classic, *Forbidden Planet* was loosely modeled on Shakespeare's *The Tempest*. Walter Pidgeon's guided tour of the place: https://www.youtube.com/watch?v=HHXfMjp2zqI

149   **after the manner of crabs and crickets:** Lewis Mumford, op cit.

      enters the very marrow of the partially developed mind: Cf. Michel de Montaigne, "The softer and less resisting the soul, the easier it is to impress anything on it. . . . That is why children, the common people, women and the sick are more readily led by the nose." (*Essay 27*)

150   **a gold rush with all the problems that entails:** Paul Spudis, author interview.

      the weasel under the cocktail cabinet: An interviewer once asked Harold Pinter what his plays were about; he replied thus and regretted it ever after. The line, which he later said meant exactly nothing, was enshrined in some quarters as the key to his work.

      replace our bones with carbon-titanium: Andrea Mills et al., *Big Questions* (DK Publishing, 2011).

      scrub our bloodstreams with nanobots: See, e.g., Jacopo Prisco, "Will nanotechnology soon allow you to 'swallow the doctor'?," *CNN* (January 30, 2015).

151   **effective immortality:** A phrase regularly propounded by futurist Ray Kurzweil in discussions of the Singularity, loosely defined as the moment when man and machine become indistinguishable.

    declared goal to live 700 years: Darren Orf, "BTA Panel: Peter Diamandis Q&A," *Popular Mechanics* (October 22, 2013).

    Death: I don't accept it: as quoted in Katie Ryder, "A Theory of Love," *The Paris Review* (April 19, 2013).

    (see endnote for complete list):

    I take about 250 pills of nutritionals a day . . . For boosting antioxidant levels and for general health, I take a comprehensive vitamin-and-mineral combination, alpha-lipoic acid, coenzyme Q10, grapeseed extract, resveratrol, bilberry extract, lycopene, silymarin (milk thistle), conjugated linoleic acid, lecithin, evening primrose oil (omega-6 essential fatty acids), n-acetylcystein, ginger, garlic, l-carnitine, pyridoxal-5-phosphate, and echinacea. I also take Chinese herbs prescribed by Dr. Glenn Rothfeld. For reducing insulin resistance and overcoming my type 2 diabetes, I take chromium, metformin (a powerful anti-aging medication that decreases insulin resistance and which we recommend everyone over 50 consider taking) and gymnema sylvestre. To improve LDL and HDL cholesterol levels, I take policosanol, gugulipid, plant sterols, niacin, oat bran, grapefruit powder, psyllium, lecithine and lipitor. To improve blood vessel health I take arginine, TMG and choline. To decrease blood viscosity I take daily baby aspirin and lumbrokinase. I reduce inflammination by taking EPA/DHA and curcumin. I have dramatically reduced my homocystein level by taking folic acid, B6 and TMG. I have a B12 shot once a week and take a daily B12 sublingual. Several of my intravenous therapies improve my body's detoxification: weekly EDTA and monthly DMPS. I also take n-acetyl-l-carnitine orally. I take weekly intravenous vitamins and alpha-lipoic acid to

boost antioxidants. I do a weekly glutathione IV to boost liver health. Perhaps the most important intravenous therapy I do is a weekly phosphatidylcholine IV, which rejuvenates all of the body's tissues by restoring youthful cell membranes. I also take PtC orally each day and supplement my hormone levels with DHEA and testosterone. I take I-3-C, chrysin, nettle, ginger and herbs to reduce the conversion of testosterone into estrogen. I take a saw palmetto complex for prostate health. For stress management I take l-theanine, beta-sitosterol, phosphatidylserine and green tea in addition to drinking 8 to 10 cups of green tea itself. At bedtime I take GABA and sublingual melatonin. For brain health I take acetyl-l-carnitine, vinpocetine, phosphatidylserine, ginkgo biloba, glycerylphosphatidylcholine, nexrutine and quercetin. For eye health I take lutein and bilberry extract. For skin health I use an antioxidant skin cream on my face, neck and hands every day. For digestive health I take betaine HCl, pepsin, gentian root, peppermint, acidophilus bifodobacterium, fructooligosaccharides, fish proteins, l-glutamine and n-acetyl-d-glucosamine. To inhibit the creation of advanced glycosylated end products I take n-acetyl-carnitine, carnosine, alpha lipoic acid and quercertin.

—From Kurzweil's book, *The Singularity Is Near.* The total seems to have fluctuated through the years.

152 **Our astronaut breathes like a Peruvian:** A term coined by Toby Freedman and Gerald Lindner in "Must Tomorrow's Man Look Like This?," *Popular Science* (November 1963).

Optiman: Ibid.

the universe is saturated with our intelligence: Cf. Firesign Theater: "Everywhere he went, man dropped a great load of knowledge, forming a rich compost . . ." (*We're All Bozos on This Bus*, 1971)

launching off from Earth like a spaceship: as quoted in Kliph Nesteroff, "Destination Subconscious: Cary Grant and LSD," (March 21, 2010), http://blog.wfmu.org/

freeform/2010/03/his-girl-lsd-the-cary-grant-experience. html. Starting around 1959, Grant took LSD some 100 times.

won't create a consciousness: Antonio Regalado, "The Brain Is Not Computable," *MIT Technology Review* (February 18, 2013).

153 **or claim to be:** Lisa Eadicicco, "Bill Gates: Elon Musk Is Right . . .," *Business Insider* (January 28, 2015).

summoning the demon: as quoted in Javier David, "Rise of the Machines!," *CNBC* (October 25, 2014).

keep an eye on what's going on: Justin Moyer, "Why Elon Musk is scared of artificial intelligence . . .," *Washington Post* (November 18, 2014).

Bill Gates is doing the same kind of thing: Eadicicco, op. cit. According to the article, "more than a quarter of Microsoft Research's attention and resources are focused on artificial intelligence."

154 **And where goes common purpose then?:** To use a more extravagant metaphor: Think of the Singularity as a major appliance, like a refrigerator. Let's say for the sake of argument that it will work, but to plug it in you've got to transport it across a giant gorge on a narrow suspension bridge made of rope and planks. Even if you're somehow inching it across—no small feat—you're constantly subject to outside interference from things like changes of weather or little monkeys scampering out and getting in your pants. As happened to Charlie Chaplin: www.youtube .com/watch?v=AhrNFfDeWak

unintended consequences or "revenge effects": Edward Tenner, *Why Things Bite Back: Technology and the Revenge of Unintended Consequences* (Knopf, 1996).

155 **86 billion neurons of the brain:** Bradley Voytek, "Brain Metrics" (May 20, 2013), https://www.nature.com/scitable /blog/brain-metrics/are_there_really_as_many.

156 **uniformly through enemy facilities:** All quotations in this paragraph from John M. Collins, *Military Space Forces: The Next 50 Years* (Brassey's Inc., 1989).

Real gunfights!: My thanks to astronomer Edward Gleason of the University of Southern Maine for alerting me to this line of inquiry.

six times farther: As expressed by the equation $R = v2 \text{ Å}\sim \sin (2a) / g$. Kate Becker, "What happens to a bullet fired on the moon?"(April 9, 2004), http://curious.astro.cornell.edu/physics/44-our-solar-system/the-moon/general-questions/105-what-happens-to-a-bullet-fired-on-the-moon-intermediate.

157 **shoot yourself in the back:** Natalie Wolchover, "What Would Happen If You Shot a Gun in Space?" (February 22, 2012), www.livescience.com/18588-shoot-gun-space.html.

5,300 mph: Bruce McClure, "Escape Velocity on the Moon," http://www.idialstars.com/evmc.htm.

158 **lunar foxholes will shield people better:** John M. Collins, op. cit.

as yet nonexistent—propulsion systems: Guy Gugliotta, "US Planning Base on Moon to Prepare for Trip to Mars," *Washington Post* (March 26, 2006).

159 **survived scalding heat and pitch darkness:** Marc Kaufman, *First Contact: Scientific Breakthroughs in the Hunt for Life Beyond Earth* (Simon and Schuster, 2011).